5

NOT AN EASY WIN

ALSO BY CHRYSTAL D. GILES

Take Back the Block

NOT AN EASY WIN

CHRYSTAL D. GILES

RANDOM HOUSE  NEW YORK

Text copyright © 2023 by Chrystal D. Giles
Jacket art copyright © 2023 by Xia Gordon

All rights reserved. Published in the United States by Random House Children's Books, a division of Penguin Random House LLC, New York.

Random House and the colophon are registered trademarks of Penguin Random House LLC.

Visit us on the Web! rhcbooks.com

Educators and librarians, for a variety of teaching tools, visit us at RHTeachersLibrarians.com

Library of Congress Cataloging-in-Publication Data
Name: Giles, Chrystal D., author.
Title: Not an easy win / Chrystal D. Giles.
Description: First edition. | New York: Random House, [2023] |
Audience: Ages 10 and up. | Summary: Nothing has gone right for twelve-year-old Lawrence since his Pop went away, but after getting expelled from school for fighting he discovers the world of chess and things begin to change.
Identifiers: LCCN 2022003925 (print) | LCCN 2022003926 (ebook) |
ISBN 978-0-593-17521-7 (trade) | ISBN 978-0-593-17522-4 (lib. bdg.) |
ISBN 978-0-593-17523-1 (ebook)
Subjects: CYAC: Chess—Fiction. | Recreation centers—Fiction. |
African Americans—Fiction.
Classification: LCC PZ7.1.G5529 No 2023 (print) |
LCC PZ7.1.G5529 (ebook) | DDC [Fic]—dc23

The text of this book is set in 13.5-point Bembo.
Interior design by Ken Crossland

Printed in the United States of America
10 9 8 7 6 5 4 3 2 1
First Edition

FOR MY GRANDMOTHER HENRIETTA,
THE CENTER OF MY VILLAGE

CHAPTER ONE

Expelled. I was pretty sure that meant I was being kicked out of school—forever.

Principal Spacey didn't even bother to look at me when he handed the sentence down. I'd been warned after my last fight: "The next time you walk into my office will be your last," he'd said.

That was just four weeks ago, when I'd had six fists pounding my head into the pavement. I wouldn't call that a fight; it was more like a beatdown. This time it was just two fists and one foot. I was able to escape before it got too bloody—I even threw a couple of punches of my own. I had actually become pretty good at taking hits: my skin had gotten harder to hurt. But like Mr. Spacey said, it didn't matter who'd started the fight, just that it had happened. And *it* had happened to me one too many times. Even if Billy Jakes had gotten into just as many fights.

Mr. Spacey treated our school like it was some kind of jail. He was the warden instead of the principal, always walking around talking about maintaining law and order. He couldn't wait to get rid of me (and only me).

I could hear the frustration in Ma's voice from my spot outside Mr. Spacey's office. "Please give him one more chance," she said. "Please." I hated hearing her beg, especially since it wouldn't help.

This *was* my last chance.

I'd tried to get Ma to transfer me to another school after the last fight. Andrew Jackson Middle School was no place for me. I never fit in here, and I never would.

I sat there listening to him explain to Ma that I was a distraction and he wouldn't tolerate my disregard for the rules he'd put in place for his school. He dismissed her (and me) by saying, "That is all."

Ma held her head up high and walked out of his office, past me in the waiting area, past the pale-faced office ladies, and out the front door. I slow-walked behind her, waiting to hear how this was all my fault.

"Now what you gonna do?" Ma asked me after we were out of earshot of the nosy office people.

Me? What about them? I shrugged. I didn't know what I was gonna do and I didn't care.

Honestly, I hoped I'd never see this place again.

Ma went on talking, more to herself than to me. "You wasting my gas, comin' back and forth up here to this school. . . ."

And just like that, this was my fault. I looked forward and kept walking toward the parking lot. With each step, I winced. A rib shot was the worst kind of pain—way worse than a shot to the face.

When we got to the car, I hesitated. Ma was in a fussing mood, and I'd have to listen to this all the way to Granny's house.

"Get in!" Ma yelled. Her calm was completely undone now. "You're twelve years old . . . too old for this!"

I went over to the passenger side of the car and waited for Ma to open the door. That door didn't open from the outside anymore. It had just stopped working one day. No one knew why, but that was probably my fault too.

"The only job you have is to go to school, and you can't even do that!" Ma started in again. "If you aren't in school, you'll have to find some kind of way to help out. Your granny won't let you sit around the house all day."

"I can just leave," I said under my breath.

"Where you gonna go?" Ma spat out.

I didn't have an answer.

I stared out the window into the gloomy air—the gray skies stared back. She was right: I was trapped. We rode in silence for exactly twenty-two minutes before we turned off the main road onto bumpy Polk Lane. Granny's street wasn't a dirt road, but it wasn't smooth pavement, either. After lots of driving on and no fixing, it was mostly broken-up pieces of asphalt now.

Ma pulled off the cracked road into Granny's gravel driveway and turned the car off.

She let out a deep breath.

"Look, Lawrence, this ain't all on you. Life is hard, and we've had a double dose of hard lately." Ma's voice was softer now—her version of an apology. I knew I'd never get the real thing. Ma wasn't the apologizing type.

Whenever I did something wrong, I had to apologize. I wasn't sure why adults didn't have to.

For a moment, I'd forgotten about my stinging left eye. It would double in size if I didn't get ice on it soon. I sat in the thick air of Ma's car waiting for her to ask about it or at least see if I was okay.

Two long minutes passed—silence.

"All right, let's just go in and get it over with." Ma sighed. "If she says something, we'll just say it wasn't your fault."

It wasn't *my fault!* I wanted to yell out. But I knew it wouldn't matter. No one cared about what had really happened. No one cared that I'd had a huge target on me since the day I started at that school.

Everyone just looked at me like I was the problem.

CHAPTER TWO

Granny stood in the front doorway watching as me and Ma climbed the steps. Her hand was on her hip, and her lips were fixed to start a fire.

"Mama, before you start, it wasn't his fault," Ma began. "Them kids at that school have been picking on him since he got there." I wished she'd said that to Principal Spacey. Or to me.

"Tracey, you make so many excuses for that boy," Granny said, ignoring me.

Ma brushed past Granny and went inside.

Following Ma's lead, I slid by Granny and headed straight to the back bedroom. I slumped on the bed and tried to take advantage of the quiet before the house filled with running feet and screaming kids. My little sister, Nikko, and our twin cousins would be here soon.

I peeled off my ripped hoodie and tossed it on the

floor. JOHNSON C. SMITH UNIVERSITY was printed on the front in faded gold letters. That hoodie was what had started the fight that got me expelled. Maybe I could blame Uncle Bennie, Pop's brother—he'd given me the hoodie for Christmas last year.

Not that it had anything to do with them, but the kids at Andrew Jackson used it as a reason to start messing with me. "What kind of college is that?" I think that came from Colson Sims, or maybe Brett Masters. Their yappy voices spun around in my head. "Where'd you get that shirt?" "He probably stole it." "You ain't going to college." "He don't even know what college is!" I wasn't about to let that slide.

Andrew Jackson was full of white kids who always got their way. At least it seemed like it to me. Sometimes they needed a lesson in how to treat people. Sometimes was today.

"Lawrence, get in here and help with dinner," Granny called.

I sighed and headed to the kitchen, where Granny stood waiting for me.

We were having salmon patties again. Yuck. The stinky smell smacked me in the face as Granny drained the liquid from the can and emptied the fish into a bowl. My stomach turned.

"Your hands better be clean," she said, not even looking at me.

Washing my hands in Granny's kitchen sink was a huge no, so I walked back through the living room, down the short hall, and into the bathroom.

I passed Ma on the way. She was slumped on the couch, trying to get a nap after her shift at the diner. I tried not to look at her.

At the sink, I let the water pour over my bruised hands. The cool burn felt like everything else in my life—numbing and mismatched.

"Mix in the mayo and egg, and make the patties while I boil the rice," Granny said when I got back.

"Yes, ma'am."

I cracked the egg and dumped it and the mayo into the bowl. I smashed the gummy, fishy-smelling mixture with my hands and started forming the mound into patties, imagining that they were burgers instead. I would have loved a juicy hamburger—I couldn't remember the last time I'd had one. Since we'd moved in with Granny, we'd eaten salmon patties every single week, usually on Wednesdays.

Knock, knock, knock!

Loud banging on the front door shook the house.

Ma got up from her spot on the couch and opened the door. I peered around the wall separating the kitchen from the living room and peeked out the screened front door.

It was Mr. Bob from Bob's Diner, where Ma worked,

and he looked mad. He always looked mad. He and Ma didn't really get along, and he had this thing of stopping by Granny's house to let Ma know when she'd done something wrong. Which felt like something a boss shouldn't do, but Mr. Bob did what he wanted.

Ma went outside to talk to him on the porch. I tried to be super still and not make a sound while I struggled to figure out what Mr. Bob was saying to Ma. She was standing with most of her weight on her back leg, leaning away from him. He had gone from talking to yelling—my heart thumped in my chest.

A few minutes later, Ma came back inside and slammed the door shut.

The heart thumping slowed down when I heard Mr. Bob's car door shut and tires spin extra hard on the gravel.

"He's probably making a big fuss about her leaving work early to go pick you up," Granny said from in front of the stove.

I should've known she'd blame me for that, too.

CHAPTER THREE

I was used to being blamed for stuff, especially living at Granny's house. Maybe 'cause I was the only boy, but it was usually my fault that we were out of milk, or eggs, or cereal. Saturdays were the worst, mostly because then I had to listen to Granny complain all day about what I was or *wasn't* doing right.

That made Saturday my least favorite day of the week. I'd moved a lot over the past couple of years—three times, to be exact. With every move, I found a new day of the week to hate.

It was a wet Monday two years ago when Pop left for good. He was there; then he wasn't. I knew the fussing with Ma had gotten worse, and sometimes Pop didn't come home at night . . . but even that had become pretty normal. Then one day he was gone. For a whole month, I hated Mondays. I'd wake up every Monday morning with a dull ache in the pit of my stomach, just enough pain to remind me that I might never see Pop again. He came back home after four Mondays, but not to stay. And then Monday became the day he'd come and go.

Then I hated Fridays. It was a sad Friday one year ago when we moved to Uncle Bennie's. We were so behind on the rent after Pop left that the landlord kicked us out of the only house I'd ever lived in. I came home from school to find an eviction notice tacked to the front door. I grabbed the notice off the door and stuffed it into my pocket before Nikko could see it.

I spent the rest of that day wishing for a miracle. Maybe Pop would come running around the corner to save us—take us to some huge house with four bedrooms and three bathrooms.

I'd always wanted to live in a house with three bathrooms. I'd actually have been okay with even two big bathrooms plus that little bathroom for when people visit. I just wanted one for myself so I wouldn't have to share with Ma and Nikko. But nah, that only happened to the white kids on TV. We waited till it was dark that horrible Friday, after the neighbors were asleep, and we moved out that same night.

We only lasted a few weeks at Uncle Bennie's. I knew when we got there it wouldn't work. Imagine me, Ma, and Nikko crowded in Uncle Bennie's one-room apartment. Everything, including the bed, was in one room, which was a disaster from the start. And then he and Ma stopped getting along. It was this weird big sister–little brother energy, even though Uncle Bennie was Pop's brother—no way we could last.

Then I hated Wednesdays. It was a rainy Wednesday that same year when we left Charlotte and moved to Larenville. We drove two and a half hours to Granny's house in the middle of Nowhere, North Carolina. Like, really, there was nothing around for miles—no corner stores, no parks, nothing.

The smelly goo between my fingers reminded me it was Wednesday again. When I was done making the patties, Granny cranked the heat on the stove burner nearest me and started to brown the mush. I leaned against the wall and waited for her to finish. Granny didn't allow sitting in her kitchen until all the cooking was done, which was why Ma never came in the kitchen while Granny cooked. Ma wasn't the cooking type, never had been: she took orders and served customers at the diner, and she said that was enough. Before we moved in with Granny, dinner was microwavable or came from a greasy bag.

"Your mama told me they kicked you out of school," Granny said as she flipped the patties in the pan.

"Yeah, I got in too many fights." I looked down at the

floor. No use in telling her I couldn't make it into the building without Billy or Colson starting with me.

"Well, a man that don't work don't eat. The Bible says that," Granny said. "So you better find a job cutting grass or something."

"Yes, ma'am." I wished I *could* work—then maybe we could eat something other than canned fish and rice.

"And you may as well put some ice on that eye before it swells. It'll be bigger than your head soon."

The stomping of feet on the steps rescued me from another Bible sermon. The kids were home. I rolled some ice into a towel and crept out of the kitchen to meet them at the front door.

"Lawrence has a black eye!" my little cousins sang when I opened the door. Iris and Ivy sang-said everything at the same time, like an R&B duo. Probably a twin thing.

"Are you okay? What happened?" Nikko asked, wrapping her arms around me.

"I'm fine, Nik," I said. "See, it's not that bad." I moved the ice from my eye to give her a peek.

"You got beat up again?" Iris asked. I ignored her and walked back into the house.

Nikko and the twins were eight and in the third grade. They went to Andrew Jackson Elementary, which was one street over from the middle school. Aunt Carmen, Ma's sister, used Granny's house like a boarding school during the week. She wanted her kids to go to the "good school," so they stayed with Granny and went to school from her house. The "good school" meant the white school.

Andrew Jackson Elementary and Middle were *almost* all-white schools. The kids were white, the teachers were white, the principals were white—even the walls were white. In the year I'd gone to the middle school, I'd only counted six other Black kids. At my school in Charlotte, Black kids had outnumbered the white kids by like ninety percent—for real, it was like the exact opposite here.

There were two other middle schools in Larenville, where most of the Black kids went. One was too far from Granny's house, and the other was the Booker T. Washington Center for Excellence in Education—a charter school for excellent kids, I guessed. You could only get into Booker T. with special permission, so we were stuck at Andrew Jackson.

That left me trying to hide in the middle of an almost all-white school. *Uncomfortable* isn't even the right word to explain what it's like to be surrounded by mean staring eyes and too-loud whispers. There's something about being constantly reminded that I'm different that makes me extra edgy, like a revved-up engine ready to spin out.

At least Nik had the twins. They kept her company

and had her back at school, something I couldn't do, since I went to the middle school. At least I used to.

The kids crowded around the TV to watch cartoons while Granny finished dinner. I squeezed in next to Nikko, catching a whiff of her shea-coconutty hair grease. I wished I could escape to the back bedroom until it was time for dinner, but Nik'd be worried about me. And she already spent too much time worrying—something an eight-year-old shouldn't have to do.

When dinner was ready, me and the kids huddled together on a blanket in the middle of the living room floor. It was our dining room table. I liked to think of it as an indoor picnic rather than us not having a table big enough to fit everyone.

"Move your leg!" Ivy yelled.

"No, you move," Iris snapped back. "My leg was here first."

"Both of y'all move!" I said. My eyes dared them to say something else.

Dinnertime was when the kids lost their minds—it was my job to make sure they kept their hands and feet away from each other and kept food off the floor. I had learned to eat really fast so my hands were free to break up fights.

Ma and Granny were hunched over the two-person table in the kitchen. The only sounds floating between them were their fork clanks. Ma and Granny didn't talk much—to each other, anyway. I figured they were too alike—or too different, depending on the day—to have anything to talk about.

I used my fork to slide the salmon patty from one side of my plate to the other. I couldn't force myself to eat another canned-fish pie. I actually missed eating microwaved meals almost as much as I missed Charlotte. I'd have given anything for a single-serve Stouffer's lasagna right now. Nikko actually liked the patties—she had gobbled hers down and was working on the rice. I wondered who'd come up with the idea of putting fish in a can anyway. Someone who didn't have to eat it, that's who.

Stomach rumbles eventually beat out my stubbornness: I stuffed the mush into my mouth—and swallowed. Yep, just as gross as last week.

• • •

Most nights I slept on the living room floor on a pallet made of blankets, but tonight I propped myself up on Granny's good couch. I'd suffered enough rib shots to know that lying on the floor wouldn't work. I just hoped Granny wouldn't wander through the house and catch me. She had rules about her couch: naps were cool, but overnight sleeping was not.

The dark quietness while everyone slept was the only thing I liked about Granny's house. Out here in the country, everything was super still at night. I only ever heard singing crickets or sometimes a howling dog. Not like in Charlotte, where you could hear a car horn blaring or some random fireworks at any time.

Nights in the living room were when my mind had time to slow down. Ma and Granny had the little rooms off the front of the house, and Nikko and the twins were stuffed into the larger back bedroom. When Iris and Ivy went home on the weekends, I slept in the room with Nikko. I usually didn't mind trading in the quietness of the living room for the low purr of her snoring. I kinda liked it.

I stared into the black air and listened to the quiet. I tried not to worry about tomorrow, about what I'd do all day and how I could stay out of Granny's way.

CHAPTER FOUR

A low, off-tune voice crawled into my ears: "Precious Lord, take my hand, lead me onnnnn. . . ."

Granny was up.

I jumped off the couch quick, forgetting that my ribs had taken a beating the day before. After a few slow, shallow breaths, I folded my sleeping blankets and crept into the hallway to put them away in the closet.

Ma was awake too. I could hear her talking with Granny about something. ". . . Mama, I know. All this has just been too much on him. I'll figure it out." Granny was the only person I knew who could fuss and sing church hymns in alternating breaths.

Ma didn't sound completely sure that she'd figure out whatever Granny was on her about.

"That's his problem; you do too much for him. He's almost a man, Trace. He needs to find his own way."

"He's only twelve years old, Mama. That's not almost a man!" Ma said.

This was about *me*? I didn't feel like a man at all—not even a little.

"He's acting like it, getting kicked out of school, fighting and going on," Granny said.

"I'm going up there today to some kind of hearing, seeing if they'll let him go back," Ma said.

A hearing? Like a trial? I bet Mr. Spacey'll be there.

"If they don't, they'll set him up in an alternative learning environment. It's April; school will be out in two months anyway. Don't worry, Mama—just give me a couple days," Ma continued.

"He ain't got a couple days. He can't stay here all day watching TV," Granny said, and I knew she meant it.

Maybe Ma would wait a couple of days, but I wouldn't. I'd figure this out for myself. Granny didn't have to worry about me.

I slipped into the back bedroom, careful not to wake the kids, grabbed a change of clothes, and headed into the bathroom.

Fifteen minutes later, I was dressed and bent over a bowl of Oat Os and milk. Granny would make her way to the kitchen soon to start cooking breakfast for the kids, and I wanted to be gone when she did. I rinsed my bowl and snuck out the front door.

I took in the cool spring air—perfect hoodie weather.

It'd rained overnight, leaving the air feeling and smelling fresh. Maybe this was a sign that today would be better than yesterday. Either way, I'd avoided Granny, so that was a good start. I stepped out onto the damp grass and started walking. I wasn't sure where I was going, but I had to go somewhere.

I fished Pop's old iPod out of my hoodie pocket and popped in my earbuds. The scratched-up machine played music and was like an iPhone but without the phone. It was the only thing Pop had left behind that was usable. He'd loaded all his favorite songs on it, and even though it was old-school music, listening to it made me feel closer to him—a spin of the soundtrack to his life, back when things were good.

A song by OutKast, Pop's favorite rap group from Atlanta, pumped into my earbuds, and it was like Pop was there walking with me. Back home, Pop always had music playing in the background, and now I could almost hear him rhyming along with it. It's weird how music can do that—take you right to another place.

I reached the end of Granny's yard and turned left. There are only a few houses on Granny's street, nothing like our neighborhood back in Charlotte, where I could never take off down the block without being noticed.

I walked on the edge of the road heading toward town.

The rappers rhymed about Atlanta having the coolest dudes on the planet, and I wished I was there—I wished I was anywhere but here. Cars zipped by me as the sun started to rise, and when a couple of school buses filled with screaming kids rode by, I pulled my hoodie down to cover my face and kept walking.

The roaring howl of a truck engine and the whipping sound that followed made my stomach flop. I knew what it was before it passed me. I kept my hoodie low and looked straight ahead when it drove by. A Confederate flag stood tall from a pole attached to the bed of the truck.

The huge X in the middle of the flag was like a warning sign. "Pure evil" was what Granny called it. She'd told me anybody waving that flag had evil in them. It made me scared to think what that evil could do—could do to me. Granny also said that if I was alone and saw someone waving that flag, I better say a prayer and hope to make it home safe. I'd learned in third-grade social studies that the Confederates, who were trying to keep people enslaved, lost the Civil War, so I never understood why people still wanted to wave the losing flag. But I did what Granny'd told me and said a quick prayer.

That flag gave me another reason to hate this place. Not saying I'd never seen one in Charlotte, but they weren't a regular thing, not like here.

After trekking through gravel and broken-up road for two miles, I finally reached the main road, Highway 34, which led to Larenville's downtown area. Downtown is nothing special, just one block of stores and restaurants, the police station, and the courthouse. At the rate I was walking, it would take another hour to get there, but the walk would be better than being at Granny's.

While I walked, I thought about why Granny didn't like me—or, if she did, why she didn't show it. I'd asked Ma once after we moved here, and all she'd said was, "Lawrence, don't worry about Mama—she's stuck on how she thinks things are supposed to be. That's a *her* problem, not a *you* problem. She'll come around."

I couldn't remember being around Granny much before we moved in with her. She'd never been to Charlotte to visit us, and we'd only come to see her twice a year, on Easter and Christmas. I did remember her being nice enough—not extra sweet like some grannies, who knit you fuzzy hats, but nice enough. Then, when we moved in, she just stopped being nice at all—to me, anyway. With Nikko and the twins she was fine. Maybe screamy little girls were her thing, 'cause I sure wasn't.

I figured she didn't want to be bothered with us. Ma said Granny was used to her life the way it was, and then we stormed in and messed things up. By *us,* I figured she meant *me.*

Pop's music thumped in my earbuds, and the playlist was halfway through its second rotation by the time

I reached the Piggly Wiggly grocery store. It was right on the edge of downtown. My feet hurt, my left side ached, and my throat burned for something to drink.

I slid my hoodie off, popped out my earbuds, and walked toward the store. It was mostly white women in the parking lot, loading their cars with groceries. I passed a woman on the way inside pushing a baby in a stroller. I must have really scared her, because she cut the corner hard enough to lean the stroller on two wheels. I didn't know what it was—maybe my black eye, or my black skin, or maybe just me. I let her pass, and I headed straight to the drink cooler at the closest register.

I grabbed a Tahitian Treat and laid it on the belt. The cashier's name badge said KAYLA; she looked just a little younger than Ma and stared at me like she knew I wasn't supposed to be there.

"Shouldn't you be in school?" she asked, one of her eyebrows lifted up.

I thought about saying, *I'm never going back to that school,* but I said, "Not today," hoping she wouldn't ask me any more questions.

Instead of running the drink over the belt, she handed it to me, winked, and waved me toward the exit. I wasn't sure if I could trust that she was being nice to me, so I quick-stepped out the door.

I'd barely hit the exit before I cracked open the soda

and drank the sweet red goodness. I'd gulped half of it by the time I reached a little park across the street.

I found a seat on a swing and finished my drink, watching the people in town walk from one place to another. That made me wonder how people had so many places to be, especially in this little town.

The big clock in the center of Main Street pointed to ten o'clock. On a normal day I'd be in second period, trying not to be noticed, and then on the school bus by three p.m., on the way back to Granny's house to wait for Nikko and the twins to get home. Nikko must have wondered why I wasn't home and where I was when she woke up this morning.

I put my earbuds back in and pushed play on Pop's iPod. The thing is, Granny had never liked Pop. Maybe that was why she didn't like me. I'd listened to Ma try to prove for years to Granny that Pop was a good man, which he really was. Everyone said so. His old boss at Walmart, where he worked when I was in second grade, gave him an EMPLOYEE OF THE DECADE T-shirt even though he'd only worked there a year. Pop wore that shirt so much, the words completely faded off.

And Pop could fix anything—cars, TVs, my remote-control toys—anything. He was basically the fix-it man for our old neighborhood in Charlotte. He was super strong, too, like Hulk strong. Nobody messed with Pop, which meant nobody messed with me, either.

Every Easter and Christmas, Pop would stay home when we visited Granny. I think he was trying to keep everybody happy. But then he up and left, so maybe Ma was wrong and Granny was right. Either way, Pop was gone.

I leaned back in the swing, kicked my legs up, and propelled myself high into the air. The wind wrapped around me. I kicked again and again, and for a moment I felt like I was flying. Flying over this stupid town—to a place with less meanness, a place where things were good, and the bad things weren't my fault.

CHAPTER FIVE

People strolled around downtown all day. I moved from the swing to the bench right next to it, and back to the swing. I kept thinking someone would come and run me off, but I was mostly invisible—only twice did someone throw me a weird look. And the nice lady inside the store let me use the bathroom when I went back inside to buy a snack.

I started my walk home when the big clock pointed to four o'clock. My steps were a lot faster than earlier in the day so I could make it back to Granny's house by six-thirty, when we usually ate dinner.

• • •

Nikko jumped up to give me a hug as I slid through the door. Granny, Ma, and the twins were in front of the TV watching *Jeopardy!* That meant I'd missed dinner.

"Where you been all day?" Ma asked. She had enough irritation in her voice to let me know to keep my answer short.

"Just walking," I said.

Ma motioned for me to follow her into her room. I hoped this wouldn't be another blame-Lawrence session.

"I went to the hearing for your expulsion," Ma said.

I could tell from her twisted brow it hadn't gone well.

"They aren't letting you go back to school. You'll be finishing the rest of seventh grade from home."

A little streak of relief filled my insides; I didn't want to go back.

"To be honest, I think they'd already made the decision before I got there," Ma said.

They probably had. They'd never wanted me there anyway.

"There's an online system set up for what they call 'alternative learning.' A teacher will assign you work, and you'll turn in everything online," Ma went on. "You'll still be able to move up to eighth grade. . . ." I had already stopped listening after she said I wasn't going back. I could finish the work with no problem, as long as I was done with that place.

"That's all I know for now," Ma said. Her voice sounded tired.

I felt a little guilty that Ma had to deal with me getting into trouble. I'd never had any school problems in Charlotte. Not like I was the smartest kid in class or anything, but I did have *some* friends. And I didn't start getting into fights until we moved here. Now it seemed like all I did was get into trouble.

Granny didn't turn an eye in my direction when I walked back into the front room; she and the twins just kept watching TV.

"I fixed a plate for you," Nikko said with a nervous grin.

"Thanks, Nik." Even when I couldn't do anything right, Nik still looked out for me. She got that from Pop. She was a fixer like him.

"Go in there and eat so my kitchen can be clean before I go to bed," Granny said without looking up.

Nik had left my plate in the microwave. I knew what was on the plate before I'd even looked at it. *Beanie-weenies.* We always had baked beans mixed with chopped hot dogs on Thursdays. I pushed the quick-heat button on the microwave and watched the turntable spin. When I saw exactly two seconds left on the clock, I grabbed the door handle and pulled out the plate before the timer went off. Granny wasn't happy about having a microwave in her kitchen, and she got especially irritated when the timer beeped.

I settled in at the two-person table in the kitchen and dug in. Before I could take my last bite, Nik came to sit with me.

"Ma said you can't go back to school." Worry lines creased her forehead. Nik had the smoothest light brown skin, like the color of wet sand at the beach. Her dark brown hair was brushed up into two ponytails pinned on each side of her head above her ears. Ma had curled the hanging ponytails into loose spirals. She looked like Ma with her hair like that—and not like me at all.

My hair was deep black and my skin was barely lighter. Pop's friends used to call him Midnight, and when I was around they'd call me Lil' Midnight. I guess midnight was as dark as you could get. I never minded my complexion much until people back home started saying there was no way Nik and I could be related, with me being as dark as the night sky and her being as light as the sun is yellow. Pop always told me to ignore that noise.

Nik stared at me with her big round eyes, waiting for me to answer. "Yeah . . . I got in another fight," I said.

"But they was picking on you, right?" Of course Nik understood.

"You know Principal Spacey don't care about none of that."

"But you could tell Ma, and she can tell him."

I felt bad 'cause Nik really thought Ma could save me. I knew she couldn't. Not sure when I'd stopped waiting for someone else to make things all better, but— for real for real—waiting to be rescued would have you waiting a long time. I figured people saw you how they saw you. Principal Spacey saw me as the problem—Ma couldn't fix that.

"It's too late for that, Nik. Don't worry—it's already April. Plus, they're going to let me do school online," I said, trying to sound convincing.

I wasn't sure if it worked, but she smiled. "Does your eye hurt?"

"Not really. It feels better than it looks."

That made her laugh a little. Then she got serious again. "Lawrence, Granny said you have to get a job or find somewhere else to live, but since you not old enough to work . . ." Her voice trailed off, low in her throat. Then she started again. "You not gonna leave like Pop did, right?"

I tried to think of a good answer. I wished I could give her that safe feeling we'd had when Pop was around. All I could come up with was "No. I ain't going nowhere, Nik."

CHAPTER SIX

The next morning, before Granny could start her gospel hymns, I had already gotten dressed, eaten my Oat
Os, and washed my bowl.

I pulled on my hoodie and stepped outside. I had
nowhere to go. And I didn't want to walk all the way
back to the park in town. Granny's voice replayed in
my head: *He can't stay here all day watching TV.* I'd have
to figure something out until the school got me set up
online. I popped my earbuds in and turned right at the
edge of Granny's yard.

The sun was crawling to its usual position in the sky
when I reached Mr. Dennis's house. I could see a light
on inside. Mr. Dennis was Granny's closest neighbor,
even though you couldn't see his house from Granny's
front porch.

Mr. Dennis was old—older than Granny, I guessed,

but a lot nicer. His house was also a lot nicer than Granny's house. It was twice as big, and he had a porch lined with enough rocking chairs for every one of us to have our own when we came to visit. I'd spent lots of afternoons rocking in a chair while him and Granny talked about Mister So-and-So or Sister So-and-So. Really, it was mostly Granny talking while he listened; he never said much himself.

Without even thinking about it, I found myself walking up Mr. Dennis's driveway, onto his porch, and tapping on his front door. Brownie, his German shepherd, barked loud enough to make me jump back before the door creaked open.

"Sit," Mr. Dennis said to Brownie, and then greeted me with a crooked smile.

I popped out my earbuds and said, "Hey." I didn't mean to say *hey,* but I didn't know what else to say. It didn't make sense for me to be at his front door on a school day, but there I was.

"Hey, Lawrence. Mae or Tracey need something? . . . Want to come in?" he said.

"No . . . yes."

Mr. Dennis's heat must've been turned on, because inside his house felt like an open oven. It was extra toasty, warm enough that I had to cough to catch my breath. I followed him to a plaid couch, where he had a wooden tray with legs positioned in front of one end. He took a spot behind the tray and pointed for me to sit beside him.

He lifted a spoon from a bowl on top of the tray and loaded clumpy grits into his mouth. Mr. Dennis was nicer than Granny, but Granny definitely made better grits.

He finished his bowl of grits and dry-looking toast before he turned to me and said, "Why you not in school?"

I couldn't think of a better way to say it, so I just said, "I got kicked out—for good."

"Well, they had no business sending you to that Andrew Jackson school anyway. That place is made for them, not us. How would you do well when you don't have anyone around that looks like you?"

That was the most I'd ever heard him say at one time. I didn't know exactly what I was supposed to say, but I figured he was on my side, and that made me feel good.

"So I guess Mae won't let you stay in the house all day," he said. He definitely knew Granny.

"A man that don't work don't eat," I said, trying to copy the way Granny had said it.

Mr. Dennis slow-smiled like he understood, but he didn't say anything. And since he didn't say anything, neither did I. We just sat there in the quiet of a too-hot room on a now-itchy couch.

Maybe I should've gone to the park.

Then he moved his tray on legs into the kitchen, grabbed his hat, and told me to come with him. I had no idea where we were going, but it wasn't like I had anywhere else to go.

We went out the front door and climbed into his faded light blue pickup truck and started down his driveway.

We turned left on Union Road, the opposite direction of downtown, passing by a row of trailer homes and a junkyard full of rusty cars. I'd never gone this way before; in fact, I'd never been any place in Larenville besides school, Piggy Wiggly, CVS, the diner where Ma worked, and church when Granny made me go.

After a few more minutes, we turned down a dirt road and stopped in front of a wide, flat brick building. Mr. Dennis parked the truck and got out. I guessed I was supposed to follow, so I jumped out too and trailed behind him to the entrance of the building.

CARVER RECREATION CENTER was etched on a sign tacked to the front door. Even though I was glad not to be stuck with Granny or wandering around downtown, I wasn't sure this would be any better. And I wouldn't have called *this* a rec center.

Mr. Dennis took us in through a side door and then through another door marked OFFICE.

"What is this place?" I asked. Mr. Dennis *had* to be too old to work somewhere. I wasn't sure what he used to do, but I figured he must be retired from it.

"I've been coming here every day for the past ten years," Mr. Dennis said, not even answering my question.

I looked around the dim office, wondering what kind of work he did here. And with who.

"But nobody's here."

"It's only seven. Junior comes in at eight. Linda will stop by with lunch at twelve, and the kids will file in after school about three," Mr. Dennis explained. "We have an hour to get the chairs and equipment out." *A whole hour?* Clearly, he took his time doing everything.

I followed Mr. Dennis out of the office and into the large, open room that looked like a school gym. There was a basketball court up front. We put out a row of chairs along the left side and a rack of basketballs at the end of the court. Then we moved on to the section of the room with the Ping-Pong table. We put out balls and hand paddles and a row of chairs against that wall too.

I still didn't know if I'd have called it a rec center, but it was starting to feel a little less like a warehouse.

Next we went into a small room that must have been the lunchroom. Stuffed inside were two tables, a mini refrigerator, and a microwave. Mr. Dennis had me put four chairs at each table.

Then we went into another room at the back of the rec center. It was mostly empty except for two card tables in the middle. We set a chair at opposite sides of each table, and we lined all four walls of the room with extra chairs.

"Why we putting all these chairs in here?" I asked. "Who gonna sit in all these chairs?"

"You sure ask a lot of questions," Mr. Dennis said.

That was my sign to shut up, so I did and went with Mr. Dennis to the front of the building.

It must have been eight o'clock, because a man the size of an NBA basketball player walked through the front door. Junior was much taller than I'd pictured for a guy named Junior. He gave Mr. Dennis a pat on the back and turned to me and said, "Why you ain't in school?"

Telling a stranger my business felt weird, but I told him anyway. "I got kicked out."

"This is Mae's grandson," Mr. Dennis explained. "Lawrence, this is Junior."

"Hey, Mr. Junior," I said.

"I ain't nobody's mister. Just call me Junior." He smiled, showing a dull gold left front tooth. "What you do to get kicked out of school?" Junior asked.

"Um . . ." I didn't want to get into all the fighting, or how I was suddenly always in trouble, even if it wasn't exactly my fault. "I, um . . ."

"Don't worry about it. Happens to the best of us," Junior said, flashing that gold tooth at me. "I'm surprised I even graduated; I spent my whole senior year in detention or at home." He laughed. "How long you get kicked out for?"

"For good." That sounded worse than it had in my head. "I mean, they said I can go back next year."

Junior looked at me like I had burned the school down, or something just as bad. Then he smiled again and said, "Well, we're stuck with you, huh?"

"I guess so?" *I hope so.* This place didn't seem too bad, and it would give me something to do. I hoped I *could* stay here instead of being fussed at all day by Granny.

Junior gave me an up-and-down look and reached his hand over to give me a pat on the back. That pat meant yes, and the question in my mind about where I was supposed to be felt less like a question now.

"You'll have to earn your keep," Mr. Dennis said as he turned and walked toward the lunchroom.

"So, what is this place?" I asked Junior.

"It's a recreation center—didn't you see the sign?" He grinned a little and said, "We're the only county-funded before- and after-school center in town. One hundred percent owned and operated by yours truly." Junior pointed at himself and then at Mr. Dennis, who was now on the other side of the room. "We don't have any kids before school right now, but it's a full house after school lets out. You'll see."

"Walk around. Get used to the place," Mr. Dennis added as he and Junior disappeared into the lunchroom.

I grabbed a basketball and tossed it at the rim. *Clank*.
I was no good at sports, especially basketball. I'd never
even been on a team before. When I was little, Ma
had said the rec league teams were too expensive and
there was no need getting my hopes up about playing
with a ball for a living. Even Pop agreed that there was
no use in wasting time playing when I could be doing
something more useful with my hands. So when the
kids in my neighborhood in Charlotte played three on
three, I usually just watched.

I threw the ball toward the rim for a while longer,
then joined the men in the lunchroom. They were
talking about their high school days. At exactly twelve
o'clock, Ms. Linda showed up with corned beef sand-
wiches and potato salad for us.

"Linda, this has to be the best potato salad in Larenville," Junior said, going for his third scoop.

"My mama's recipe," Ms. Linda said, smiling at Mr.
Dennis. "Just potatoes, eggs, mustard, mayo, and spices—
none of that weird stuff, like raisins."

I'd never had potato salad with raisins in it, and seeing the look on Ms. Linda's face, I didn't want to.

"Dennis, you've had your fair share of Ms. Emma's
recipes, haven't you?" Junior said. He laughed before
he could even get the question out.

I was thinking Ms. Emma had to be Ms. Linda's
mom, which meant . . .

"Don't start that," Mr. Dennis said, shooing at Junior's laugh.

That made Ms. Linda laugh too.

What a weird twist the day had taken. I showed up at Mr. Dennis's front door and now I was hearing the old man's secrets. It was kinda like when Ma and Aunt Carmen talked about growing up in Larenville and all the guys they'd crushed on. I'd honestly never imagined Ma liking any other guy but Pop.

I listened to the men talk some more, and when I heard the familiar squeal of school-bus brakes, I knew the kids were here.

A flurry of brown faces that looked from Nik's age all the way up to my age busted through the front door of the rec center. I finally knew who all the chairs were for. A little spark jumped inside my chest when I saw that I'd have somebody to hang with for the first time since leaving Charlotte. At least I hoped I would.

I leaned against the far wall of the basketball court and waited for everyone to file in.

"Daaang, your eye black!" a boy yelled out, pointing in my direction.

"Shut up, Deuce!" a girl said, pushing his shoulder.

"Keep your hands off me," Deuce said to the girl. "And you see his eye—it is black."

" 'Bout black as your face!" another boy said to the girl. Her skin was just a bit lighter than mine.

"The blacker the berry, the sweeter the juice," the girl snapped back.

I'd heard that line in one of Pop's old-school songs.

Deuce busted out laughing and said, "You probably got that out of one of those books you be reading all the time." He was tall and dark-skinned with a bald fade. And I could tell he and the girl went back and forth like this all the time.

The girl rolled her eyes at him and walked toward me.

She stretched a long, thin arm in my direction and said, "I'm Twyla. What's your name?"

Twyla filled up the whole room with her sureness. I liked her already.

"Lawrence," I said, shaking her hand. Which seemed like what I was supposed to do. *Right?*

"Don't worry about them. They don't know how to act around people."

I knew better than to say anything, so I just nodded and let a little grin hang on my face. I couldn't even remember the last time I'd smiled, and there I was looking silly after just meeting her. Twyla, a name I'd never heard, and it fit her just right.

"So, you met everyone!" Junior said, walking up behind me. "This here is my son, Theodore Bryce, but we call him Deuce."

"Dang, Daddy, why you gotta tell him my whole name?" Deuce said.

"'Cause I named you. You should be proud of the family name."

Deuce didn't smile. I could tell he didn't like me. I didn't care much—most people didn't like me, not right away, anyway. Any friends I'd ever had took me a long time to get. When I complained about not having enough friends, Pop always said, "Real recognize real." I still didn't really know what that meant, but I guessed I'd rather have a couple of real friends than a bunch of people who just pretended to like me.

I grabbed a chair against the wall, sat, and watched the other kids play. Some stayed on the basketball court; some moved over to the Ping-Pong tables. The little kids were standing in a circle cracking jokes. Deuce and a couple of others were in a corner, freestyling over a beat that bumped through someone's phone. Rhymes bounced between them like they were creating a song.

After a while, I popped in my earbuds and pretended to listen. I was really watching Twyla. She sat against the opposite wall with her legs pulled up to her chest. Her eyes looked down at a book resting on her knees. The zigzag pattern braided into the top of her head stared at me from across the room.

I watched her for the next hour as she sank deeper into the book. Every now and then, she laughed a little or smiled at something between the pages, but mostly she kept an even pace as she flipped the page every ninety-three seconds.

Maybe more than an hour had passed, because Mr. Dennis interrupted my gazing to have me help him put the chairs away. And then parents started coming in to pick up their kids. It was my job to empty the trash cans, wipe down all the tables (even if no one had used them), and sweep the lunchroom. By the time I was finished with all that, the kids were gone, including Twyla.

Mr. Dennis walked around to inspect my work, and when he was satisfied, he flicked off the lights inside the rec center. While he locked up, he told me to take a walk around the whole building and make sure nothing looked out of place.

I really had no idea what I was looking for, but like Granny said, a man that don't work don't eat.

CHAPTER SEVEN

On the ride back to Mr. Dennis's house, I thought about how Deuce (which means "two") was really a third. Right? If Junior (his dad) was a junior, that would mean Deuce was Theodore Bryce III. So why was he called Deuce?

Then I thought about Twyla and how she'd kinda defended me. Or maybe she hadn't, but it had felt like she did. And I wondered what book she was reading—what could hold her attention for so long when all that noise was going on around us?

Instead of Mr. Dennis dropping me off at Granny's house, he pulled into his own driveway. "Thanks for letting me come along," I said. What I really wanted to ask was *Can I come back again?* But I chickened out.

"Ask Mae and Tracey if you can come back Monday. I'll see you at six-thirty a.m. sharp."

A small bubble of happy floated inside me and I hollered, "Okay!"

I was halfway down Mr. Dennis's driveway when I remembered I wasn't completely free from school.

"I have to keep up with my schoolwork online. . . . Is that okay? It shouldn't take long to get everything done."

"A man that don't work don't eat," Mr. Dennis said, and walked into his house.

I guessed that meant it'd be okay.

Nik had left the door unlocked for me. She and the twins were spread out on the picnic blanket in the living room, stealing food off each other's plates while cartoons blared in the background. Fork clanks echoed from the kitchen.

"Come get your plate while your food is still warm," Ma called out.

I stood in the doorway, not sure whether I should ask now or later about going with Mr. Dennis next week.

"Go wash them hands. Don't bring that outside dirt in my kitchen," Granny said.

I scrubbed the outside off my hands, went to get my plate off the stove, and sat with the kids on the blanket.

"Granny said you found a job," Nik whispered as I took my normal spot beside her.

"What?" I whispered back. "A job?"

"With Mr. Dennis . . ." Nik looked at me with one eyebrow raised. "He called earlier."

"Yeah, I helped him at the rec center. . . ." I didn't even finish my thought. I couldn't figure out if Granny had done something nice. Either way, she hadn't looked so mean when I came into the house, and I liked that.

On Fridays, we ate spaghetti—which was the best of the weekday meals. And mine was still hot. I dug my fork into a heaping plate of pasta and sauce, and for the first time in a long while, I felt like I had done something right.

CHAPTER EIGHT

Aunt Carmen and Ma looked like they could be twins like Ivy and Iris. They were the same height, had the same yellowy-brown complexion, and even wore their hair the same way. Ma called Aunt Carmen her *almost* twin because they were born a year apart. Not only did they look alike but they acted alike, too (except that Aunt Carmen was a lot funnier than Ma).

Besides being funnier, Aunt Carmen had a fancy office job two towns over, while Ma had to deal with mean Mr. Bob at the diner. She said the tips from the customers were good but that was where the good stopped.

When we lived in Charlotte, Ma was the manager of Cajun Queen—a real restaurant with reservations, white tablecloths, and desserts like bourbon bread pudding, which she brought home some nights to me, Nik, and Pop. Ma was a lot happier then.

"If you belong to me, be in the car in five minutes!" Aunt Carmen called from the front door.

Sometime between dinner and bedtime was usually when Aunt Carmen came to get the twins and take them home on Fridays. Today their pickup time was probably too close to bedtime for Granny's liking.

"Don't come in my house making all that noise," Granny grumped from the couch.

"I love you too, Mama," Aunt Carmen said. She moved from the door to the couch in one quick motion and planted a kiss right on Granny's cheek.

"I don't know where your lips have been," Granny said, wiping off the kiss.

Ma and Aunt Carmen busted out laughing, and I cracked up inside.

Granny didn't like to be touched. Aunt Carmen was asking for it.

"Ivy, Iris, let's GO!" Aunt Carmen called out again.

The twins and Nik came running from the back bedroom in one three-headed blur.

"Can Nikko come home with us?" Iris asked. "For a sleepover?"

"Pleeease," Ivy added.

"Can I, Ma?" Nik asked.

I could tell Ma was waiting on a signal from Aunt Carmen on whether she wanted to be bothered with three eight-year-olds overnight.

"Nikko can go," Granny said.

And that was that. Granny had made the decision for everyone.

• • •

After Nik, the twins, and Aunt Carmen were gone and Granny was in bed, me and Ma stayed up late watching old episodes of *The Fresh Prince of Bel-Air.* It was Pop's favorite show, and I could tell he was on Ma's mind, because every time Will did something silly, she'd shake her head like it was Pop sitting there with her instead of me.

I really liked having Ma all to myself, which I hardly ever got.

In this episode, Will and Carlton were getting dressed up to go to a party.

"Did you and Pop do fun stuff like go to parties before I was born?" I asked.

Ma smiled before I could even finish the question.

"Sometimes . . ." She stopped like she was taking herself back there. "Your pop *cannot* dance." Ma laughed. It was true: I remembered him two-stepping at Uncle Bennie's graduation party—it wasn't a good look. Ma went on. "When we did go to parties, he walked around talking to everybody the whole time."

"So what did you do?"

"Dance!" Ma said. "I'd dance with anyone beside me or near me, or I'd drag your pop onto the dance floor for a song if I couldn't find anyone else." She shimmied her shoulders a little to show me her moves.

I wanted to hear more about her and Pop and the fun they used to have, but Ma turned back to the TV, and I watched her smile slide away. I didn't think Ma liked telling stories about her and Pop. Pop's stories were better anyway. He might not have known how to dance, but he knew how to tell great stories.

Once upon a time there was a boy called Midnight. His skin was dark as the night sky. He always started the exact same way. *And he had a thing for a golden girl who lived up the street.* He was talking about him and Ma.

Ma moved from Larenville to Charlotte right after she finished high school. Ma always talked about how she'd prayed for a reason to move out of small-town Larenville to a big city. She'd gotten a job as a hostess at a fancy hotel on her first day in Charlotte. Pop must have spotted her as soon as she moved into his neighborhood, because he always talked about how he loved her from the moment he laid eyes on her.

After the fourth episode of the show was done, Ma clicked the TV off. "You're so much like him, you know?"

I got the feeling that wasn't really a question, so I didn't say anything. I was just happy she still thought about Pop—I knew I did.

CHAPTER NINE

"Precious Lord, take my hand, lead me onnnn. . . ."

Oh shoot, Granny was up! It was 6:07 on Monday morning. I had twenty-three minutes to get to Mr. Dennis's place.

I rushed into the bathroom, got dressed, and was slurping my Oat Os when Ma walked into the kitchen.

"Hurry and get out of here. And don't mess this up," she said. "Oh, and a teacher from your school will be by the rec center today to drop off your laptop and get you set up for the online portal. Please show her you're doing better."

"Okay, Ma," I said, but I wasn't sure how I was going to do that.

I poured the last of the cereal and milk into my mouth. A single milk-soaked piece missed my mouth and left a wet spot on my shirt. *Great.* There was no way I could change my shirt *and* be on time. I knew I'd rather impress Mr. Dennis than a teacher from Andrew Jackson, so me and my milk stain bolted for the door.

Brownie must have smelled me coming, because I heard barking, and then Mr. Dennis swung the door open before I could even knock.

"Six-twenty-nine, right on time," he said, glancing down at his watch.

Right on time? I was a whole minute early.

Mr. Dennis must've finished his lumpy grits before I got there. He grabbed his hat and then we were on our way to the faded blue truck.

The blue truck was old—probably as old as Mr. Dennis—and had an empty spot where the radio should've been. I started to put in my earbuds but stopped; Granny said it was rude to have those things stuck in your ears in front of other people. So the only sounds between me and Mr. Dennis on the way to the rec center were his quick, low breaths and the wind coming in through the loose seal around the passenger-side window.

When we pulled up in front of the rec center, Mr. Dennis turned to me and said, "Mondays are busy. We have to do everything we did on Friday, plus set up the chessboards. The kids have a weekly chess match right after school."

"Chess? Like checkers but with black and white squares instead of red?"

I guessed that was a silly question, since Mr. Dennis didn't even answer; he just hopped out of Old Blue. That was what I'd named the truck that day on the way to the rec.

We got right to work. I put out all the chairs while he stocked the balls and equipment. When I was done, he called me over to help set up the chessboards in the back room. The question about checkers must have really irritated him, because he said, "Chess isn't the same as checkers; chess is all about what's up here," and pointed to his temple.

Uh, okay. I hadn't been trying to bother him with that question—I'd just thought both games were the same. Or at least kinda the same. There'd been a chess club at my school in Charlotte, but I'd never thought about joining or learning to play. No one I knew played.

I watched while Mr. Dennis fixed up the boards. He set each piece on a black or white square. He was almost done when Junior joined us in the back room. The two sides of the board were set up exactly alike. Even the little horses were turned in the same direction.

Instead of hanging out in the lunchroom like they had on Friday, Mr. Dennis and Junior hung out in the chess room to have their morning talk and play the game. They sat at one table on different sides of the chessboard, and I found a chair against the wall beside them. I listened a little, but mostly I watched the board and how each of them paused for a few seconds before moving a piece.

There did seem to be a lot more thinking than playing. Junior's face was all screwed up even though Mr. Dennis's was calm.

I couldn't tell who was winning, but as the game went on, Mr. Dennis had more pieces on the board, and his pieces were closer to Junior's side of the board, so I guessed he was doing better. Then Junior moved his horse piece three squares in one turn and wiped out one of Mr. Dennis's pieces.

"Gotcha, Dennis!" Junior laughed.

Mr. Dennis didn't even look up at Junior, which made me think talking wasn't allowed. He just stared at the board, trying to figure out his next move.

"It's getting good now," Junior said, reaching over to tap my leg.

I didn't know what *getting good* meant, but after Mr. Dennis moved his little castle piece two spots and grabbed up one of Junior's pieces, Junior leaned in close to the board. They traded moves back and forth, and after a really long time of nothing much going on, Mr. Dennis said, "Check!" Junior picked up his tallest piece and moved it over one spot. Mr. Dennis called out "Check" again. Junior looked straight-up stuck. He was cornered and had no place to move. Then Mr. Dennis said, "Checkmate!" and it was all over.

The game had taken a whole hour, and I couldn't figure out what had happened except that Junior's tallest piece had been put in time-out and then knocked over by Mr. Dennis. What I did know for sure was that chess was *not* checkers.

CHAPTER TEN

We spent the next few hours in the chess room. Mr. Dennis won three games. Junior won zero.

With all the watching I'd been doing, I had figured out that the short pieces with round tops that were lined up on the first row could only move one spot at a time. The castle pieces could move any number of spaces and could move backward and forward, but only in straight lines. The horses moved in an L shape and could jump over other pieces, and the pointy-topped pieces moved in a diagonal line. The two tallest pieces—the king and queen—did the least amount of moving, but lasted to the end. I liked the queen best, mostly because she could move all over the board in any direction and could move more than one space at a time. The king lasted to the very end but could only move one space at a time. So really, the queen did the work while the king stayed pretty still—which was weird, but honestly seemed to make a lot of sense.

The queens in my life worked hard too. Ma was always tired after her shift at the diner, and Aunt Carmen said her job didn't pay enough for all the things she had to put up with.

I was happy when Ms. Linda called out to let us know lunch was here. My stomach was grumbling and I was tired of watching pieces slide across the board.

"One of the ladies from your school left this for you," Ms. Linda said.

"For me?" That wasn't the smartest thing to ask—I was the only person she could've been talking to—but I figured the school would have sent someone to maybe ask me some questions, not just to drop stuff off. I took the laptop and a small stack of papers from Ms. Linda.

"Said her name was Ms. Foxx and to call the number on this paper if you have any questions."

"Okay . . ." Ms. Foxx was one of the ladies from the office at Andrew Jackson. They couldn't even send a real teacher. I didn't feel so bad that I hadn't put on a clean shirt for her.

I wasn't one of Ms. Foxx's favorite students. She was always frowned up when I walked past her into

Mr. Spacey's office. No wonder she'd left the laptop and instructions with the first person she saw and kept going. So much for showing her I was doing better.

• • •

After lunch, I headed to the basketball court instead of back to the chess room with Mr. Dennis and Junior. There was only so much chess watching I could take in one day. I popped in my earbuds and turned the volume up high.

Pop's music blared into my ears. The choir singing at the end of the song reminded me of this one church I used to go to with Pop. The choir would sing church songs but with a nice beat, and sometimes one of the robed men would step out in front of the other singers and break out in a flow. It *was* gospel rap, but still, it wasn't bad—way better than anything at the old people's church Granny dragged us to sometimes. The music at Granny's church was long and draggy, the kind of vibe that put you to sleep. Pop's church was the exact opposite.

Pop wasn't a churchy guy, but he did like to go sometimes. He told me it made him feel better about the bad stuff he'd done when he was young. I wasn't sure what he'd done that was so bad, but at least he felt sorry enough about it to get on good terms with God.

It was funny how Pop used church to make him feel better and Granny used church to find new reasons to make us feel bad. On the Sundays she didn't make us go to church with her, she'd come home late in the afternoon and give us a mini sermon about what she'd learned.

This week the sermon was from Ezra 8:22. Granny had opened her Bible to the chapter and verse, lowered her voice, and read aloud: "'God's power and wrath is against all who forsake him.'" A chill ran over my skin—*wrath* sounded like the kind of word Mr. Spacey would use. Granny told us to think about what that verse meant. When she was gone, I reread the verse. The first part of it said: *The hand of our God is upon all them for good that seek him.*

That part sounded way less scary than the part Granny read.

I guess I was like Ma—churchier than Pop but less churchy than Granny. I didn't think of God as a mean kind of guy, but when Granny talked about him, I wasn't so sure.

Nik was just happy when she got to go to children's church with Ivy and Iris and draw pictures of shepherds and rainbow sheep. I thought more about that verse of Granny's and laughed to myself. I was sure Pop would have hated living with Granny as much as I did.

That made me miss him even more.

The screeching of bus brakes brought me back to the rec center. The kids were here. That meant Twyla was here.

I popped out my earbuds and sat up straight in my chair. I crossed my left leg over the right one; then I switched and put the right one over the left one. I stood up. I couldn't figure out what to do with my arms, so I crossed them behind my back and leaned against the wall. "Act regular," I whispered to myself.

The little kids ran in first, the older boys next, and then the older girls. Last, Twyla strolled in, talking to a girl who had to be her best friend. Maybe she wasn't her best friend, but they were whispering and giggling like Nik did with Iris and Ivy—who'd probably have loved it here at the rec.

Instead of everyone running straight to the basketball court, they lined up their book bags near the door and went to the chess room. Deuce and his friends hurried past me without saying a word.

I was still leaning against the wall when Twyla and her friend came my way.

"Hey," Twyla said. "Lawrence, right?"

I couldn't believe she'd remembered my name.

"Um, yeah. Hey." I concentrated on sounding normal. "Where's everybody going?"

"Mondays we have a mock tournament to practice

for the big chess tournament," Twyla's friend said. "I'm Kendra, by the way."

"Hey, Kendra," I said. "What big chess tournament?"

"It's this tournament that kids from all over the state go to," Twyla explained. "Corey Stitt and Alicia Cole went two years ago with Mr. Dennis, and they play on the high school chess team now. You play?"

"No, I mean, kinda . . . sometimes," I lied.

"You have to be pretty good to get a shot at the board, but you should come watch."

Just what I needed, more time staring at those black and white squares, but because I was happy for the invitation I said, "Sure."

Almost every chair in the chess room was already filled. Four kids had taken seats at the boards. Twyla and Kendra squeezed into an empty spot near the door, leaving me to stand awkwardly in the corner. Somehow that was where I always ended up: standing awkwardly in a corner.

"Let's get ready to start," Mr. Dennis announced from a seat he'd put between the two tables. He had a little timer in his hand, and a pad and pencil, I guessed for keeping score.

"Go!" Mr. Dennis called out, and it was on.

Both games started at the same time, and a blur of brown fingers and black and white chess pieces slid across the boards. Two of the younger girls, Jada and

Shayla, played against each other at one table, and they were good. They had already collected a few of each other's pieces within the first couple of minutes. Deuce played at the table beside them, against a boy who looked a little scared. Deuce's moves were quick and clean. He used the horse to hop over the other kid's pieces in back-to-back turns. I didn't know if the kid knew he was gonna lose, but I did. After watching Junior get smacked around, I knew what losing looked like and felt like. I'd lost enough battles myself to know.

The kids played a lot faster than Junior and Mr. Dennis had earlier, and neither game took that long. Because the girls' game had ended first, Deuce (the winner of his game) had to move to the other table to play the winner, Jada. Then two new players filled in the seats at the empty table.

The next games went by a little slower. Deuce won again, and the other game ended in a draw, which meant that no one won before Mr. Dennis's timer beeped. Because there was no winner, Mr. Dennis called a new challenger to the table with Deuce.

Twyla walked calmly over to the seat across from Deuce. She put her black pieces on the squares and gave Mr. Dennis a nod. Compared to the flow of the last few games, Deuce and Twyla moved like snails. Twyla calculated each move before she slid her pieces across the board. For the first time, I saw Deuce sweat a little. A thin row of wet lined his upper lip as he hunched over the board.

Twyla looked normal—cool, even—as she twirled a braided piece of hair between her fingers.

Their game moved so slowly that some of the younger kids were starting to squirm. When Deuce's queen made its way to Twyla's side of the board, his lips curled into a slight smile. But every time he tried to get into check position, Twyla used her queen to block him. It became a battle of the queens. And even though things were moving in slow motion, it was definitely the most exciting thing I'd seen at the rec. When Deuce tried to use one of his small round pieces to protect his queen, it didn't work. Twyla used that mistake to close in on the few spaces left around Deuce's king. And just like that, Twyla said, "Check." Then, right after: "Checkmate."

Deuce pushed his chair back from the table in a huff, then stormed past everyone and out the door. At that moment, I realized Twyla was the queen of chess.

CHAPTER ELEVEN

On the ride home from the rec center, all I could think about was Twyla and how amazing she was. She'd not only stood up to Deuce, but she had beaten him at chess in front of the whole rec center. She was pretty and smart. There was no way she liked me, but she did at least speak to me, *and* she'd remembered my name. That had to count for something.

Plus, she had invited me to watch the chess tournament. *You have to be pretty good to get a shot at the board, but you should come watch.* A real invitation—it didn't matter that the rest of the rec was watching too.

And right then I knew—I didn't want to just watch. I'd get good enough to get a shot at the board.

I'd need to gather up the nerve to ask Mr. Dennis to teach me how to play. If nothing else, it would get me a seat across the table from Twyla. I had to start somewhere.

Mr. Dennis pulled Old Blue into his driveway and eased his body out. He was halfway across the porch when I stopped being chicken and asked, "Hey, Mr. Dennis, can you teach me how to play chess?"

He turned around slowly and said, "Chess is a game for thinkers," and walked into the house.

So . . . no? I stood there for a minute trying to figure out what Mr. Dennis had meant.

I had no idea if he was saying I wasn't a thinker or that maybe I needed to turn my thinking up a notch. And I needed Mr. Dennis to get me there. I spent the short walk back to Granny's house thinking about how to convince him to help me.

When I didn't see Ma's car parked in Granny's driveway, I knew something was wrong. Living with Granny had made us all take on a routine. Granny was up by six-fifteen every morning (even on Saturday); Ma was up by six-thirty, and she got the kids up. Everyone was dressed by seven and done eating breakfast by 7:20. When I was in school, my bus came at 7:27, and the kids were loaded onto their bus by 7:40. I rode twenty-five minutes to school, mostly over bumpy old roads, before we pulled up at Andrew Jackson.

Andrew Jackson Middle let out at two-forty-five p.m.,

and the elementary school let out at three-fifteen. I was home by three-thirty, Nik and the twins were home by four, and Ma came in right after that from the diner.

So when I walked up Granny's driveway at six p.m. and Ma's car wasn't there, it was a warning sign.

"Where's Ma?" I asked Nik on my way into the house.

"I dunno." She shrugged.

Granny was cooking dinner—not a good idea to bother her now. I sat on the couch next to Nik and waited.

It was almost six-thirty when Granny called us into the kitchen to get our plates. Ma still wasn't home.

"Lawrence, you sit in here with me and let the kids go on in the living room," Granny instructed.

Nik and I glanced at each other with wide eyes, but we did as we were told. Something was going on, but I couldn't get up enough courage to ask Granny what.

I grabbed my plate of chicken, rice, and lima beans and moved toward Ma's seat at the two-person table in the kitchen. I waited for Granny to sit before I did. I suddenly felt like I was facing my own kind of chess match.

Granny's fork clanked against her plate while I tried to eat as quietly as I could. With Granny right there looking at my plate, I'd have to eat every last lima bean— and I hated lima beans almost as much as I hated salmon patties. I had eaten my chicken fast, too fast, so now I was stuck with rice and limas. I tried filling my mouth with a clump of rice and sticking a single bean in the middle, like a lima bean sandwich, and it kinda worked—until I ran out of rice. That left eleven off-green-colored beans staring up at me, daring me to eat them.

Granny had eaten her beans first and was finishing her rice. I could tell the kids were up to their normal fighting by the rustling noises coming from the living room.

I couldn't wait any longer.

"Did Ma have to work late?"

"You know your mama hasn't worked late a day in her life," Granny said.

I tried again. "Did she stop somewhere?"

"No," Granny said flatly.

I was fresh out of ways to ask, so I said, "Where is she?"

Granny leaned forward in her chair a little. "Your mama got fired. She's probably wandering around town feeling sorry for herself."

CHAPTER TWELVE

Fired. Ma was fired.

No job = no money.

Will we have to move . . . again?

A man that don't work don't eat.

Does that count for women too?

I sat at the table for a long time after dinner with my mind spinning off random thoughts. The thin plastic layer between my butt and the square chair cushion stuck to my pants. It had gotten loose over time, I guessed, and stuck to whatever touched it.

I would have never known that if we'd never come to live with Granny in this backward country town.

I would have never known that if Granny hadn't invited me to eat with her at the table.

I would have never known that if Ma was here and not fired.

I listened to the TV flip from cartoons to the evening news, to *Jeopardy!*, to *Wheel of Fortune.* Then it was time for the kids to take baths and get dressed for bed.

I heard Nik ask Granny where Ma was and if I was okay. Her voice sounded small and worried. I hated that she was always so worried.

Granny whispered something to Nik that I couldn't make out.

"Night, Nik," I said from the kitchen. I forced some calm into my voice so she'd worry less.

"Niiiight," Nik, Ivy, and Iris sang. The twins outsang her, but I knew Nik—she'd forced a song just like I'd forced some calm.

I stalled leaving the kitchen until Nikko and the twins were safely in their room.

Granny was waiting for me.

"I didn't tell the kids about this, and I don't want you telling them either," Granny said. "And don't you go trying to fix nothing—it's your mama's problem to fix."

I didn't know I needed to hear that, but I was glad Granny had said it. I took a deep breath—toes deep—and asked, "Why'd she get fired?"

"Showing up late to her shifts and leaving early is what she told me."

That made me feel worse. She'd had to leave early so many times to come get me from school when she was supposed to be at the diner. My mind went right back to where it had been in the kitchen. What would we do for money now? No money meant no food, and Granny wasn't about to be feeding people who didn't work.

"I know this ain't easy, but I don't want you moping around. All of this will get figured out. I want you up early so you can be ready when Dennis leaves for the center," Granny said.

Then she stood, reached over, and patted my shoulder before she went to get ready for bed.

The guilt must've been dripping off me, 'cause Granny really seemed to be trying to cheer me up, and that was new for me.

I was alone in the dark stillness of the living room, wrapped in the fear that Ma wasn't coming home. A fear that didn't make much sense. It wasn't like she'd left us before. Not like Pop. Ma had always been there.

That fear rose a little more, though, every time I thought I heard the front door opening. But the noise was all in my mind. Ma still wasn't home.

At some point in the middle of the night, I could hear Granny's voice in a low whisper. At first I thought maybe she was talking on the phone, but then I heard her say, "Lord, what now?"

She was praying.

I rolled over on my lumpy pallet of blankets and closed my eyes. I fell asleep to the soft, concerned whisper of Granny's voice.

CHAPTER THIRTEEN

Granny was up early making a breakfast of grits, eggs, and bacon when I woke up.

I crept to Ma's room. She still wasn't home.

I had a dull pain in my gut. My mind was back to thinking that Ma might *not* come home. Pop leaving the way he did made my mind always believe the worst. It was like no matter what, I was waiting for more bad news now.

But that wasn't Ma. She'd always been there for me and Nik. Every single morning, every single night after work, no matter where we lived—Ma was always there.

Maybe she'd slept at Aunt Carmen's. . . . Yeah, that was probably it. Ma was just tired and didn't feel like facing Granny yet. She'd be home soon.

I guessed Granny hadn't slept too well, because

breakfast was done and she'd already eaten by the time I got dressed. I ate by myself at the table in the kitchen while she got the kids up and ready for school. Before I left, I gave Nik a half hug.

"Did Ma have to go to work early?" Nik asked as I was on my way out the door.

"I guess so. . . ." She didn't even know Ma hadn't come home last night. I was kinda glad Granny had asked me not to say anything. I didn't have the guts to tell Nik I had no idea where Ma was.

Mr. Dennis was waiting for me with the door open when I reached his house.

"If you're serious about learning to play chess, you need to train your mind," he said.

My brain felt blurry, and for a second I didn't even know what he was talking about.

With all this stuff going on with Ma, chess was the last thing on my mind.

We rode to the rec center in silence, like normal. We got out of Old Blue, like normal. And we put out the equipment and chairs, like normal. Instead of listening to the men chat, I logged in to the portal to get my assignments done for school. There was a video of the class crushing a can using air pressure.

I watched it and then had to answer questions about what I'd learned from the experiment. Since I wasn't actually part of the class, I just typed up what

I thought the other students had learned. I finished that assignment and answered all the questions in the computing-rational-numbers review right before Ms. Linda brought lunch at twelve o'clock, like normal.

Even though I hadn't been coming to the center that long, my routine had become pretty normal. After lunch, Mr. Dennis and Junior headed to the chess room. I followed and sat down on the far side of the room.

"Come on over here. Let's see how serious you are about learning to play," Mr. Dennis said.

He took out a board and set it up.

"You sit there." He pointed to the seat across from him.

My heartbeat started to speed up.

"Do I go first?" I asked.

"That's the problem with you young kids—always ready to push play," Mr. Dennis said, not answering the question.

"Yep. Always on go," Junior added.

"Close your eyes," Mr. Dennis said. I squeezed my eyes shut. "Now tell me how many pieces are on the board."

Oh shoot! I tried to picture the board in my mind. There were eight of the little round pieces, two castles, two pointy-topped ones, two horses, the queen, and the king.

"Sixteen!" I yelled out, with my eyes still closed.

"Wrong," Mr. Dennis said. "Open your eyes."

There was no way I was wrong. I opened my eyes and counted the pieces on my side of the board to myself. "Sixteen," I said again under my breath.

"Look at the whole board," Mr. Dennis said.

"Oh, thirty-two . . ." I couldn't believe I hadn't gotten that the first time.

"Gotta use your mind. If you're only looking at your pieces, you lose the game before you even start."

I guessed he was right, but that felt like a trick question.

Next, he told me the proper name for each piece. He held up the king first. "The king is the most important piece on the board. You lose the king and the game is over."

The queen was next. "The queen is the most powerful. The game can go on without her, but the king is weaker when she's not around."

"That's a lesson for life. We ain't nothing without a queen," Junior said.

Next were the bishops (the tall pointy ones), the knights (the horses), the rooks (the castles), and the pawns (the round ones).

"The whole point of the game is to checkmate the other king and prevent your king from being checkmated. That's it. All these other pieces are here to help you do that," Mr. Dennis said.

I'd already figured that out by watching them play.

"Okay, got it. So, when do I play?" I asked.

"Why don't you sit here and study the board and pieces awhile? You'll get a chance when I say," he said.

With that, they left me to sit and stare at the board.

I picked up the pieces and rubbed my fingers over the bends and curves. They were way smoother than I'd expected. They were much heavier, too. I pushed the pieces—black and white—all to one side of the board. There was only so much I could do by myself at a chessboard, though.

My mind started wandering.

I wondered if Ma had come home yet. I hoped so. Was there a rule about leaving your kids without telling them where you were? I bet there was. Ma had always been strict about following rules, while Pop didn't care much about rules at all. He'd always say, "Who made all these rules we're supposed to follow?" Ma had told me once that Pop "isn't a rule-breaker, but he doesn't mind bending them."

Bending rules was what had landed Pop in jail sometime after he'd left us and before we moved to Larenville. Uncle Bennie said the police pulled him over for a broken taillight—which wasn't actually broken, according to Uncle Bennie. Then the cop found an old ticket and a fine Pop had never paid. So he went to jail for something that would've never been found if the cop hadn't lied about the taillight.

Ma didn't talk much about it—actually, she didn't talk about it at all. She only told me because she knew I'd hear about it from someone in the neighborhood eventually. Ma said Pop was prone to making bad decisions, and she didn't want that energy rubbing off on me and Nik.

Before jail, Pop made sure to come by on Mondays, or call me and Nik and ask how we were or how school was going. He and Ma hardly spoke when he called—she'd just pass the phone to one of us. When Pop went to jail, the calls stopped.

Uncle Bennie said Pop was released sometime last year. But then Ma said he'd violated his probation and was back inside again. I just wished he was still around to stop by on Mondays.

Like Pop, sometimes I got stuck wondering who made these rules and were they really fair. And what made a person *prone* to making bad decisions.

I didn't talk about Pop being gone—I didn't even like to think about it, really. I guess deep down I was a little embarrassed about it. Even worse, if I thought about it too much, I started wondering if that energy Ma talked about had rubbed off on me, and that ache in my stomach came back.

Not knowing where Ma was had that pain peeking its head out again.

I popped my earbuds in to calm all the thoughts.

Some music has a rhythm you expect or patterns you can hear. Pop's music was weird—loud beats paired with quiet ones, singing in the background that didn't exactly make sense—but it did take me to another place, far away from this one. Pop said music was freedom. I'd never really thought about what he meant. But his music surely felt free. The singing, shouting, rapping in my ears didn't seem to follow any rules.

Imagine that: no rules to tell you who you are is wrong. Maybe that was why Pop loved this music so much. Listening to it made me understand him a little more, almost like I could hear him rhyming over these freedom beats too.

· · ·

I must have fallen asleep, because I was suddenly shaken by someone yanking on the cord to my earbuds. I looked up to find Deuce's mean face staring into mine.

"Why you always here?" Deuce said.

"What?" I asked.

"You got wax in your ears? You heard me." His body lurched forward, closing the little bit of space between us.

"What's it got to do with you?" I said, looking up at him.

"It got everything to do with me! My dad runs the center with Mr. D, and you don't belong here." Deuce leaned over me with his finger in my face.

"Mr. Dennis said I can be here, so don't worry about where I belong," I said, trying to act like that last line hadn't stung a little. "And get outta my face, Theodore."

Deuce snatched my earbuds from around my neck, pushed me against the table, and booked it out the door and down the hall.

"Bring those back!" I yelled. But it was too late. He was gone, and so were my earbuds.

CHAPTER FOURTEEN

I got out of Old Blue and headed to Granny's. When I saw that Ma's car was back in the driveway, I let out a breath, so relieved my stomach did a little dance that she was home.

I slow-walked the rest of the way. Not that I didn't want to see Ma—I just wasn't ready for whatever was about to change.

Ma met me on the steps and closed the door behind her.

"Hey," I said. "Glad you're back. . . ."

She smiled, which made me feel a little less nervous. She looked tired but also happy to see me.

"How was the center?" she asked.

"Fine." She had too many problems to care about mean Deuce taking my earbuds.

"So, you heard about the diner?"

"Yeah, Granny told me."

I could tell Ma felt bad. Getting fired was like getting expelled, but worse.

"Things will be a little different now, but it's going to be okay. I got a job working at the chicken plant," she said.

The chicken plant was the worst place in town to work. Before we moved to Larenville, I knew chicken had to come from somewhere, but I didn't think about where. After we got here, I started hearing stories about the chickens running wild around the yard even after their heads were chopped off.

"It'll be long hours . . . overnight," Ma said. "That means y'all will be here with Granny alone all night."

All night alone with Granny.

"You have to do your best. No more getting into trouble. I need to know things will be okay with you and Nikko when I'm not here."

She wasn't blaming me, but it was close enough. I didn't know what I wanted her to say, but this wasn't it.

"Okay, Ma. No more trouble," I mumbled.

Trouble seemed to follow me, though. First Pop left, then we had to move here, then I got expelled, now whatever problem was starting with Deuce, and this—I hoped that was a promise I could keep.

CHAPTER FIFTEEN

My chess lessons with Mr. Dennis started out slow and logical (a Mr. Dennis word). "To do well at chess, you'll have to develop logic and reasoning." He'd repeated that sentence so many times that now I knew chess was not just for thinkers but was for logic*ers* and reasoning*ers* too. Which really just seemed like understanding a pattern and knowing when to follow it and when to not follow it.

After my lessons with Mr. Dennis, I spent mornings logged in to the school portal and afternoons in the chess room alone, trying to avoid Deuce and concentrate on chess. Even though I wasn't actually playing, it was starting to make sense. Sometimes I tried to remember the moves Mr. Dennis had made that morning and figure out how I would've moved to block him if I was Junior.

I tried to trick myself into thinking I didn't miss

watching the other kids play basketball and Ping-Pong now that I was staying away from Deuce. But the rec was about more than chess, and I definitely missed talking to Twyla. If only I didn't have to see Deuce's ugly face. I couldn't bring my drama with him around Twyla—she'd think I was a troublemaker, and I didn't want her thinking bad things about me.

Now I had no one to talk to, and—as long as Deuce had my earbuds—no way to listen to Pop's iPod. I was used to being by myself, but this didn't seem fair. I hadn't started this mess with Deuce; he'd come for me. I thought about telling Junior, but that'd make things even worse, especially since I was the new kid. I'd have to deal with it on my own.

By Friday afternoon, I'd had enough of hiding in the chess room. I had decided I was going to take my earbuds back from Deuce. It's one thing to start trouble; it's a completely separate thing to defend yourself.

I walked past the Ping-Pong tables, past the basketball court, and stood in the front doorway of the rec center, waiting for the school bus to get there. A slow heat wave spread under my skin. I tried to breathe deep enough to blow it away, but every time I thought about Deuce yanking my stuff, the wave heated up.

When the bus stopped on the street in front of the center, I stepped out into the walkway, ready to confront Deuce.

He was one of the last kids to get off the bus, and when he saw me, he threw a side-eye in my direction and kept on talking to his friends. He was about to walk right past me when I blocked his path.

"Get outta my way," Deuce said, looking me up and down.

"I want my earbuds back." I tried to sound calm.

"Bwa-ha-ha," he fake-laughed. "Too late."

"What you mean, too late?" The heat wave was burning hotter.

"Too late. I threw them away."

"They weren't yours to throw away!" my voice shrieked out.

Deuce and his friends busted out laughing—some fake laughs and some real laughs, but they all made me red hot. When Deuce tried to walk around me, I pushed him with all the fire building up inside. He was lighter than he looked, or maybe I was stronger than I thought, because he seemed to fly backward in the air, and then he landed on the ground, hard. Real hard.

"Fight! Fight! Fight!" some of the kids started chanting.

Like a lightning bolt, Deuce hopped up and sent a balled fist into my stomach. I doubled over, and before Deuce could hit me again, Junior pulled him away.

Mr. Dennis was right behind Junior. He grabbed

me by the collar and yanked me toward the building's side entrance.

"He started it!" I heard Deuce yell before Mr. Dennis pushed me inside the door.

I stood nose to nose with Mr. Dennis, my back pressed against the cinder-block wall.

"We don't do that here," Mr. Dennis said.

"He stole my earbuds!" I screamed, shaking mad.

"Did you hear me?" Mr. Dennis said. "We don't do that here. I don't care who did what. We don't handle ourselves that way. *Not here!*"

Mr. Dennis turned and went out the door we had just come in. It slammed hard behind him, and I slumped to the floor with my knees pressed up to my chest.

Blood pumped fast through my body.

Here I was again: alone, in trouble, blamed for something that wasn't my fault.

CHAPTER SIXTEEN

Pop and Uncle Bennie were three years apart. Pop was older and a half head taller than Uncle Bennie.

When they were young, kids picked on Uncle Bennie a lot. He got teased for being short and wearing thick-rimmed glasses—which he still wears, but they're cool now. Pop always chased off anyone who bothered his little brother. One time he even knocked a kid flat on the ground with a single punch.

"Once upon a time there was a boy called Midnight. His skin was as dark as the night sky. He had the strength of ten lions. When he came around, the other kids knew he was about his business. That business was keeping his family safe."

"Don't go putting that in his head." Ma always interrupted that particular story before Pop could get to the part about flattening the kid who was messing with Uncle Bennie.

The first time Pop told me that story was after Tariq Porter traded me a stack of Pokémon cards for my five-dollar bill. Tariq was known for having all the new stuff—toys, snacks, whatever; if it was new, he had it. We were on our way home from school. The bus was almost at Tariq's stop.

He dangled the plastic bag filled with cards in my face. "Five dollars ain't nothing for this whole deck."

He was also known for talking a good game. And I fell for it.

We completed the trade, and before he could get off the bus, I opened the bag to find that almost all the cards were stuck together. Like they'd been wet and had dried all crusty on top of each other.

I jumped off the bus and chased Tariq all the way to his house.

His mom came to the door and made him undo the trade, but she still took his side. Said he didn't know the cards were ruined. *Yeah, right.* Then she walked me back to my house to complain to Pop about me running down Tariq. I got my five dollars back, but I'd probably be in trouble, too.

Pop closed the door behind Tariq's mom and told me the story about him and Uncle Bennie. He told me he was proud of me for standing up for myself. Later, after Ma got home, she wasn't so proud. She said chasing down Tariq could've gotten me in more trouble than it was worth.

"He was wrong," I said.

"But that wasn't the right way to handle it," Ma said.

"He was trying to do the right thing," Pop said to Ma. "We just need to work on his approach."

CHAPTER SEVENTEEN

After the rumble with Deuce, the rest of the afternoon was wasted with me sitting on the floor outside the office door, waiting for someone to come get me. Hours passed before Mr. Dennis opened the door that led into the gym and motioned for me to get up. I guessed he was really mad, because he didn't even bother speaking to me.

Most of the kids had gone for the day, and it was time to clean up. I got busy with my normal chores, looking over my shoulder every so often to make sure Deuce didn't creep up on me, just in case he was still hanging around. I was alone in the chess room when an easy voice interrupted me.

"Why you let him get you in trouble?"

Twyla stood in the doorway.

"I dunno," I said.

"He was just trying to get you mad. Can't you see that? And you fell for it."

"He took my earbuds."

"All that over some earbuds? Seriously?" Twyla shook her head.

Hearing her say it aloud did make the whole fight sound stupid, and that made me think about Mr. Dennis's trick question about the chess pieces on both sides of the board. I knew Deuce wasn't feeling me—if I'd been paying attention to the whole picture, I could've seen he was pushing me to fight. I *should've* seen this coming.

"My pop gave 'em to me. . . ." I was trying to make it sound better.

"Mr. D and Junior don't allow fighting, so you have to find a way to get along with Deuce," Twyla said. "Or you're outta here." Then she turned and left.

It wouldn't be the first time I had been kicked out of somewhere. But honestly, I'd started to like the rec center—plus, I'd promised Ma no more trouble, and I was running out of places to go.

I got busy putting the chairs away and sweeping the lunchroom, but I needed to talk to Mr. Dennis. I wanted to at least tell him my side of the story.

When Mr. Dennis was done with his paperwork, he walked past me and toward the front door of the center. He called, "Let's go," over his shoulder on the way out the door.

I slid into the passenger side of Old Blue, and we rode in thick silence the whole way to his house. When we pulled into his driveway, he paused for a minute, then said, "You and Deuce have more in common than you know."

"But—" I started.

"You have one more chance." He held up a long, skinny brown finger an inch from my face. "One. That's it."

I wanted to tell him it wasn't my fault. I wanted to tell him Deuce took *my* stuff. But I wanted to go back to the rec center more than I wanted to be right, so all I said was, "Okay," and hoped he wouldn't tell Granny.

• • •

Ma's new schedule meant she left at five p.m. to start her shift at the chicken plant at six and didn't get back home until seven the next morning. Which meant I only saw her on Saturday, Sunday, and Monday mornings—and even then, she slept a lot.

Since she wasn't home for dinner anymore, sometimes I ate with Granny at the two-person table in the kitchen and sometimes on the blanket with Nik and the twins.

But it was Friday, and for once Aunt Carmen had taken the twins back to their house straight from school, so I was happy to share the blanket with just Nik tonight. I hardly had time with her by myself, and she'd been missing Ma now that she wasn't around as much. I needed a distraction to keep my mind from wandering back to Deuce and that silly fight. And what did Mr. Dennis mean that we had something in common?

We slurped our spaghetti and watched cartoons side by side. Nik was halfway done when she leaned over and asked, "Do you think Ma will ever eat dinner with us again?"

"Sure, Nik, it's a job—it won't be forever. Don't worry," I said. "Besides, ain't I enough?"

"Yeah, and I'm not worried," Nik said. "I just miss her a little."

Like me, Nik knew what it was like to miss so many things. I wished she didn't.

I wished we could all be a normal family again. Pop, Ma, me, and Nik—like the old days in Charlotte. I pushed that thought out of my mind. Nothing was normal. And who made up what normal was, anyway?

Granny came to sit with us in the living room after the dishes were done, and just the three of us watched TV together. It wasn't nearly as weird as I thought it'd be. Granny even laughed once; at least I thought she did.

During Final Jeopardy!, the host read the answer: "Consisting of twenty-one verses, the book of this minor prophet, whose name means 'servant of God,' is the shortest." Granny called out, "Obadiah!" I yelled out, "John!" Nik yelled out, "Job!"

All the contestants on the show got the answer wrong; so did Nik and I. Of course Granny was right— she knew the Bible back to front. The fact that we were both loud and wrong made Nik giggle and me laugh, and I was pretty sure Granny giggled too.

CHAPTER EIGHTEEN

With Ma at the chicken plant all night, we mostly communicated through the trail of feathers she left on the way to her room. I heard the feathers say, *Good morning, Lawrence—love you,* and I hoped that when Ma saw them all cleaned up she heard, *Love you too.* But since "cleanliness is next to godliness," me and Ma's feather talks usually led to Granny fussing.

On Monday morning, there were no feathers to sweep up, so I ate my Oat Os, cleaned my bowl, and was waiting on Mr. Dennis's porch at 6:20 a.m. I had spent the weekend replaying in my mind what Twyla had said about letting Deuce get me in trouble. I'd never thought about it that way. I mean, after three days alone in the chess room, all I'd been able to think about was getting my earbuds back!

But after all the yelling and fighting was over, I'd

ended up in a dark hallway by myself, one inch from getting kicked out of the rec center, and I *still* didn't have my earbuds. I'd gotten played. Not because I got punched in the gut, but because I'd let Deuce get me mad.

"You're early," Mr. Dennis said when he walked out onto the front porch.

The plain tone in his voice made me feel lumpier than his morning grits.

"Yep! It's chess-tournament Monday!" I reminded him, trying to change his mood.

"You aren't ready to play, but take some time and really study each move made, and *not* made, today."

I didn't think Mr. Dennis was still talking about chess. He always used those coded messages to tell me something that had nothing to do with what we were talking about.

I climbed in the truck and we made our quiet trek to the rec center. I started my chores right away, got my schoolwork done, and then joined Mr. Dennis and Junior in the chess room. I was nervous about how Junior would feel about me. I mean, I did get into a fight with his son. But he didn't bother me at all—he greeted me with his normal gold-tooth smile.

I spent the rest of the morning watching Mr. Dennis beat the snot out of Junior in chess. I watched the moves Mr. Dennis made and even the ones he didn't make. Like, there were a few times he could have taken

Junior's pieces but he didn't. He gave him a chance to build a defense before he came in for the kill. At first I didn't understand why Mr. Dennis didn't just beat him right away, but it seemed that chess was a slow-winding game, where you had to build a strategy and execute.

The morning passed by just fine, and really, watching them play chess calmed me a little. But as the afternoon got closer, my calm insides turned into a river of nerves. I'd been in enough fights to know: the kid who got beaten up had at least a full day of getting picked on after. I was hoping that something interesting had happened over the weekend to take the attention away from me.

When kids crowded into the center, I bounced a ball at the far end of the court with my back to the door, waiting for everyone to ignore me on their way to the chess room.

I was wrong.

"What's up, Lawrence? I mean, Hulk," some kid called out.

"Yeah, you went Super Saiyan on Deuce!" someone else said.

I stopped bouncing the ball but kept my lips glued shut. *Maybe I didn't lose the fight.* Deuce gave me a death stare when he passed me. I dropped my eyes toward the floor.

Twyla came in last with Kendra. They were wearing

matching round aqua-blue purses crossed over their chests.

"Hey, Twyla. Hey, Kendra." I tried to sound calm even though my heart was pumping in overdrive.

"Hi, Lawrence," they said at the same time.

"Glad Mr. D let you come back," Twyla said.

"Yeah, me too," I admitted.

"Well, I think it was about time somebody put Deuce in his place," Kendra said.

I hadn't heard Kendra talk much, but when she did, she said exactly what she meant, just like Twyla.

"I'm going to get us a seat before the tournament starts." Kendra turned to leave.

Then it was just me and Twyla.

Sweat started to pool on my palms, and a swarm of random words buzzed around in my head. I kept trying to form a sentence, but nothing made sense. Finally, I blurted out, "I'm done fighting. I made a big deal about nothing."

"Maybe it wasn't nothing, but it wasn't worth fighting over," Twyla said.

She was right. Deuce wasn't worth it.

"I got you something." Twyla dug into her purse and handed me a small plastic-wrapped package.

"Earbuds?" I said when I unwrapped it. "Thank you."

"I had some extra ones at home. I promise I didn't use 'em."

"Even if you did, I wouldn't mind your earwax."
Oh, gross, Lawrence!

"Uh, okay. You're welcome, and maybe you can get back to listening to your beat-up old iPod," Twyla laughed. "Anyway, gotta get to the tournament."

I watched her walk away, and a wave of warm air flushed my face. If I wasn't as dark as the night air, I would've been blushing.

• • •

Twyla and Deuce were due for a rematch, and I didn't want to miss it. Deuce sat in the seat beside Junior, waiting for his turn at the board, and Twyla shared a seat with Kendra. I tried not to stare at Twyla, but I couldn't help it. She had the smoothest skin and a super-deep dimple in her left cheek. Today her hair was braided in four straight-back cornrows, and she wore little aqua heart earrings, the same color as her purse. She and Kendra whispered and laughed while they watched the two matches going on at the boards.

Jada and Lin were playing against each other. I'd seen Jada play before—and the rainbow notebook she carried around—but Lin wasn't a regular chess player; he usually hung out with the freestyling kids. He was short and light-skinned with long cornrows, and he was barely paying attention to the game. I wondered how he'd gotten a chance to play before me.

Deuce sat stiff and sour-faced in his seat, not talking to anyone. Even though he looked like his dad, Deuce didn't have the easy vibe Junior did.

Deuce must have sensed me looking at him, because he shot me an icy glare. I looked away quick, but not quick enough that we didn't lock glares for a few seconds. I surrendered and turned away before he did. I wasn't scared of him, but I kept replaying Twyla's words in my head: . . . *it wasn't worth fighting over.*

The funny thing about Deuce was, he was actually the kind of kid I would have normally liked. But whatever—if he didn't like me, I didn't like him. I had enough going on with staying out of trouble; I didn't have time to worry about making friends with Deuce.

When it was time for the final match of the day, Mr. Dennis called Twyla and Deuce over to the chessboard. Twyla strolled over in her cool way and Deuce dropped into his seat with a thud. Twyla picked the black pieces. She turned all her pieces in the right direction and gave Mr. Dennis the nod.

Twyla got off to an early lead. She collected four pawns, a rook, and a bishop from Deuce's side of the board, just like that. And, more important than the pieces she collected, she collected his confidence.

"How'd she get so good?" I whispered to Kendra.

"Mr. Dennis has been coaching her for forever," Kendra said. "Mondays have always been chess club. For a long time, Twyla and Deuce were the only ones who wanted to learn, so they just played each other over and over. The matches started getting good between them, and then everyone else wanted to play." So, really, chess club was the Deuce and Twyla Show.

Kendra went on. "Then last summer Twyla started playing online at home. She's been cooking everybody since then."

Twyla showed Deuce no mercy. She stomped her way to checkmate his king. Instead of making a big deal about it, Deuce just pushed his chair back from the table and walked out of the chess room. On his way past me, I saw a look in his eyes that I definitely knew—the look of defeat. And for some reason I kinda felt bad for him.

CHAPTER NINETEEN

The next day Mr. Dennis decided it was time for me to take my seat at the board. I'd been waiting for this for over a week. He sent me to the chess room to set the board up.

Just like Twyla, I took my time and lined up the pieces perfectly straight; then I took a seat behind the black pieces. I imagined knocking Mr. Dennis's king over with my queen. I'd send it flying across the room when I won. Well, maybe not flying, but I'd definitely knock it over.

"You sure he's ready for this?" Junior asked Mr. Dennis when they joined me.

"This is the only way he'll learn."

I'd never thought I would be a chess player—a player of anything, really. I wanted to yell, *Yes, I'm ready!*

Junior sat across from me behind the white pieces and flashed me his gold-tooth smile.

Confusion spread across my face, and before I could

say anything, Mr. Dennis said, "You didn't think you were playing me, did you?" They both laughed. And that was the start of my beatdown.

The game went like this:

Junior moved his fourth pawn two spaces forward.

I moved my fifth pawn two spaces forward.

Junior moved his left knight in a right L.

I moved my fourth pawn one space forward.

Junior moved his fifth pawn two spaces forward.

I moved my left knight in a left L.

Junior moved his right knight in a left L.

I moved my fifth pawn diagonally one space to take his fifth pawn. *My first capture!*

He moved his left knight in a right L and captured my pawn. *He set me up.*

I moved my right knight in a left L.

Junior moved his right bishop diagonally left two spaces.

I moved my second pawn one space forward.

Junior moved his knight in a right L.

"Checkmate," Junior said with a grin.

"Wait!" I called out. "How did I lose?"

"If Junior moves his knight here, you're done. Your king is trapped," Mr. Dennis said.

I moved Junior's knight in a left L, like Mr. Dennis said, to be sure. He was right—it was over. I'd made a total of six moves. I hadn't even seen it coming.

On the way home from the center that afternoon, I was still trying to figure out how I lost against Junior. I'd watched him and Mr. Dennis play for hours, and Junior never won. How'd he beaten me so easy? I'd played myself by thinking Junior would be easy to beat.

"You did well today," Mr. Dennis said as we pulled into his driveway. "I mean, you lost, but you lasted longer than I did when I first learned to play."

"For real?" I asked.

"Yep. You still have a lot of work to do, but if you're serious, I'll work with you," Mr. Dennis said. Then he handed me a small sheet of paper with a row of numbers and letters scribbled on it.

1. d4 d5 2. Nc3 e6 3. e4 Ne7 4. Nf3 dxe4
5. Nxe4 Nbc6 6. Bd3 g6 7. Nf6#

"What's this?" I asked.

"It's the moves from your game with Junior."

"What do the numbers and letters mean?"

"Each square on the chessboard represents the intersection of a number and a letter. When you get home, draw yourself a chessboard on a sheet of paper. Eight squares wide, eight squares up and down. Letter the squares from *A* to *H* across the bottom, and number the squares from one to eight on the side; then match the squares with the moves on the paper."

"Uh, okay. Thanks, Mr. Dennis."

This was way more work than I wanted to do. I'd started all this chess stuff to get an up-close look at Twyla on the other side of the chessboard, and now I had homework—plus, I was no closer to competing against Twyla. I couldn't even beat Junior.

I waited until after dinner to do my chess homework. Granny, Nik, Iris, and Ivy called out loud and wrong responses to *Jeopardy!* while I sat at the kitchen table creating a pretend chessboard. After I had drawn (and redrawn) the lines to create sixty-four semiperfect squares, I numbered and lettered the boxes like Mr. Dennis said.

"What's that, checkers?" Nik asked, now standing behind me in the kitchen.

"It's chess, not checkers. They're completely different," I said.

"Chess not checkers, chess not checkers." The twins had made up a new song.

"Looks like checkers to me." Nik shrugged.

"Yeah, but it's not. Chess is a game for thinkers," I said in my best Mr. Dennis voice.

"That sounds like something Dennis would say," Granny said.

"Yep." And then I added, "How do you know Mr.

Dennis so well? I mean, I know he lives next door, but he never comes over and . . ." As soon as the words fell out of my mouth, I wished I could stuff them back in. Granny never talked about anything personal with us, and the look on her face said she wanted to keep it that way.

"Dennis was good friends with your grandfather. They grew up together." Granny's eyes drifted past me and Nik.

I didn't remember my grandfather—he died when I was a baby—but I'd seen him and Granny in a couple of pictures she had hidden away in a drawer in the kitchen. She'd looked different then—younger, but also happier. My favorite was the one of Granny leaning on a car, looking over her shoulder at my grandfather. The sun had washed out most of the background, but I could see the happy in her eyes.

"Anyway, enough about Dennis." Granny walked over and stood beside Nik. "How're you liking chess?"

"Well, I'm no good. The other kids at the center make it look so easy." I looked down at the fake board. The truth was, I was worried I'd never get good enough to compete with the other kids.

"Anything worth having is worth working for," Granny said.

Yep, she and Mr. Dennis were friends for real, always talking in code.

...

When it was time to go to sleep, I went into Ma's empty room and eased onto her bed. Last weekend Ma had given me permission to sleep in there.

I stared at the walls for a few minutes and tried to get comfortable. Ma's bed was stiff and narrow and didn't have much bounce, but it was better than my lumpy pallet of blankets. I shifted left and right, and left again. I fluffed the flat pillow at least eight times and then folded it in half. After all that shifting, my body was finally settled, but my brain wouldn't shut up. Thoughts of Granny washed in sunlight, and Nik, Ivy, and Iris singing, and Ma chasing headless chickens, hung in different corners of my brain.

I got up and tiptoed back into the hall. I hunted through my shelf of junk in the closet. I got Pop's iPod and the brand-new earbuds Twyla had given me. Then I curled back into my spot in the middle of Ma's bed. I popped in my earbuds and drifted off into a half sleep with Pop's music in my ears and the faint smell of Ma under my nose. And for a moment, it felt like both my parents were there with me.

CHAPTER TWENTY

The cool April mornings had turned May and muggy. In North Carolina, we have something the weatherman calls humidity. It makes the air thick and hot, and you have to work harder to breathe. Old Blue didn't have air-conditioning, so the quiet ride to the rec center had turned into a *hot,* quiet ride. Even with the windows rolled all the way down, sweat started to gather under my armpits before we made it to the center in the mornings.

Since my first time at the chessboard had been a disaster, I'd used the past few days to play chess against myself, trying different combinations to win. Because I didn't have a chessboard at Granny's house, I spent mornings at the center (after my chores and schoolwork) practicing my moves while Junior and Mr. Dennis had their morning chat. I felt a little silly beating myself, but it was helping, and I had figured out how Junior beat me in just six moves.

I'd upped my nerves enough to ask Junior for a rematch. So on Friday morning I marched into the lunchroom with my head high.

"Junior, I'm ready to play you again," I said.

"You think so, do you?"

"Yes."

"Well, set up the board, young'un. Let's do it."

I quick-walked to the chess room and set the board up. I chose the white pieces this time and got myself ready to battle.

Junior didn't look nearly as excited as I was. He didn't look excited at all, but he got comfortable behind the black pieces and Mr. Dennis sat against the wall with his paper and pen. Since I chose the white pieces, I went first.

I was calmer this time. More focused, maybe, and those black and white squares were starting to look familiar. It took Junior twenty-six moves to beat me, *and* I even checked him.

I didn't win, but man, I felt good—I had Junior sweating. He'd barely won.

This was the closest thing to victory I'd felt, maybe ever. I had to tell somebody!

When the kids piled into the center that afternoon, I searched the crowd for Twyla.

The freestyle circle was gathered around her and Kendra. They were right in the middle of a flow.

Twy and Ken,
the best girls at the rec.
Act like you know,
and show some respect.

The others clapped it up for them as they walked off.

I guessed this was really a thing, especially if Twyla and Kendra were freestyling too. Not for me, but I could respect it.

I met up with them by the Ping-Pong tables.

"Twyla, you won't believe it! I almost beat Junior in chess."

"Oh . . . okay. Good job," she said, with a hint of funny in her voice.

"Honestly, Junior isn't that good," Kendra said. "I mean, even Jada can beat him."

They burst my happy bubble just like that.

"If you want some real competition, you should play in our tournament on Monday," Twyla said.

"Um, Mr. Dennis may not let me." I tried to come up with an excuse. Playing with Junior and Mr. Dennis alone was a challenge; competing in a room while the whole center watched was a whole other challenge.

"Don't worry. I'll talk to him," Twyla said.

I should've kept my mouth shut. I was nowhere near ready to battle the other kids. Especially not Deuce. I'd done a good job of avoiding him over the past week—the last thing I needed was to be inches from him across the chessboard.

"Oh, and don't worry—Deuce is too good for you to play against. You'll get paired with some of the low-end players," Twyla explained. Kendra laughed. "Wait, that didn't come out right, but you know what I mean," Twyla said.

"Yeah, no problem." Twyla could say anything and it'd be okay with me.

Twyla and Kendra sat at their favorite end of the court and pulled out their books. I got myself in the perfect position across the room to see the other kids play basketball or Ping-Pong, and watch Twyla turn pages.

I fished Pop's iPod and my earbuds out of my pocket. Now when I popped my earbuds in, I thought of Twyla. I pressed play and let the music fill my head.

"Lawrence, you want in?" Lin called out to me. Even though Lin hung with the freestyling kids, including Deuce, he seemed pretty nice and mostly did his own thing.

"Me? Nah, I'm good," I said. Ain't no way I was going to embarrass myself playing basketball with these kids, especially not in front of Twyla. Plus, Lin's team was playing against Deuce's team, so that was an extra no.

"He's too chicken," Deuce said.

He was trying to bait me and I knew it—I was paying attention to the whole board this time. I just turned up the volume in my ears and blocked him out.

"You hear me! That beat-up iPod probably don't even work," Deuce said, moving toward me. My shoulders tensed, but I locked in to the music and tried not to let him bother me.

"Ay, chill, Deuce, before we all get in trouble," Lin said.

"You better be glad my dad's in the other room," Deuce continued. "Or I would take that, too." He pointed at the iPod.

I silently dared him to try it. Pop's iPod would be worth fighting for, and Deuce would have it coming.

Deuce, Lin, and the other kids got back to their basketball game, and I tried to get back into Pop's music. But instead of cool and funky, all I heard was *He's too chicken*. This drama with Deuce had gotten my head all messed up.

I escaped to the chess room to chill out and start on my afternoon chores early.

I was stacking chairs when Twyla joined me.

"What was that about?" she asked.

"I dunno." I shrugged.

"Deuce being Deuce," she said.

"What does that mean?"

"All I know is he doesn't like new kids. So he acts tough until the new kid fights him or leaves the center."

"Well, I'm not going anywhere," I said. *I don't have any other place to go.* I wanted to tell her how badly I needed to be here, but that felt dramatic, and I wasn't sure she'd even care.

"How'd you get here, anyway?" she asked. "I don't mean to be all in your business, but Mr. Dennis didn't say. . . ."

"Um, well . . ." She'd probably find out at some point. And she *was* asking. . . . "I got kicked out of Andrew Jackson," I mumbled.

"I knew I'd never seen you at Booker T. So, Andrew Jackson was that bad, huh?"

"It was for me."

"What you get kicked out for?"

I dropped my eyes to the floor. For some reason, I felt guilty telling Twyla about all the fights I had gotten into. "Fighting," I said finally.

"You must really like fighting."

I thought she was joking, but I couldn't tell, so I said, "I only fight when I have to." Which wasn't exactly true. Some of those fights I could've walked away from.

"I'd never let someone get me to fight if I didn't want to," she said.

She was right. I kept trying to think of something not stupid to say, but I had nothing. "How is it at Booker T.?" I asked, trying to change the subject.

"It's good, I guess. Pretty much like it is here at the rec center. Except for books, teachers, and classes and stuff. All the kids that come here go to Booker T."

I thought about how different things would have been for me if I'd applied to get into Booker T. It sounded like the closest thing to Charlotte—more kids who looked and acted like me.

"Well, see you Monday. I gotta go before my mom comes looking for me," Twyla said.

"Okay, bye. See you Monday."

"And no fighting." Twyla smiled. Then she was gone.

The rest of the afternoon I stacked chairs, swept, and dumped trash, but all I could think about was Twyla's smile and how her dimple *had* to have gotten deeper since I first saw it.

CHAPTER TWENTY-ONE

I spent the whole weekend memorizing the moves from my games with Junior. I used my pretend chessboard and retraced the steps over and over.

Nik spent her weekend talking Ma's head off about a new girl in her class named Cassy. She was Nik's best friend now. Apparently she had a collection of cat headbands—she wore a different one every day. I hadn't even known Nik liked cats. Ma teased that Iris and Ivy wouldn't like being replaced. Then they both teased me about my paper board and how it was the only friend I played with. Which wasn't funny at all, *but* I had to admit it did look a little strange.

It was nice having Ma around this weekend even if she was making fun of me. But I hadn't played chess as long as the other kids at the rec, and I had to be ready on Monday just in case Mr. Dennis let me play. I was going to ask him on the way to the center.

• • •

I got up early and headed to Mr. Dennis's at 6:20 Monday morning. I was so antsy that I couldn't sit, so he found me leaning against the passenger side of Old Blue.

"Morning, Lawrence," Mr. Dennis said. "You must be ready to go."

"Morning, Mr. Dennis." I climbed inside and rolled the window down. Mr. Dennis cranked up the truck and we were on our way to the center.

"Uh, Mr. Dennis, guess what Twyla said."

After a few moments with no response, I tried again.

"Twyla said something funny on Friday."

Still nothing.

"You hear me?" I asked.

"Boy, go ahead and tell me," Mr. Dennis said, sounding irritated.

"Twyla said I should play in the tournament today. I mean, she said I should *ask* to play in the tournament today."

"And what did you say?"

"I wasn't sure if you would let me."

"So, are you asking?" Mr. Dennis raised one eyebrow.

"Yes," I said, taking in a deep breath. "Yes, I'm asking. Can I play in the tournament today?"

"You'll go in the first round. Be ready as soon as the kids get out of school."

Yes! I was in.

I got my morning chores and schoolwork done at lightning speed so I could get to the boards—maybe one day I'd need to know about misplaced modifiers, but right now I was just glad to get my class assignments checked off. Mr. Dennis and Junior played a couple of games against each other while I practiced moves by myself. I went over all the possible combinations from my last game with Junior, and I worked out three options for my starting move and for what Mr. Dennis called a counterattack.

He'd also taught me to think about the game in three parts: the opening, the middle game, and the endgame. The opening is really about the first combo of moves, feeling out your opponent, and trying to control the center. In the middle game, the battle starts. It's all about attacking and defending. It's where the most action happens. The endgame is when most of the pieces are captured and it's time to figure out how to get the win. It's also when the king becomes a fighting piece.

• • •

I was already back in the chess room when the kids loaded in. My stomach was tied in knots, and beads of sweat lined my face, but I was ready. I picked a seat in my favorite corner and waited for my chance.

Deuce was in a much better mood today—at least I thought he was; he didn't scowl at me like he had last week. He and Lin picked seats in the middle of the room, and Twyla and Kendra shared a seat near the door. When everyone was there, Mr. Dennis got us to quiet down and told us that today was free day at the tables. Anyone who wanted to play could.

I wondered if Mr. Dennis had made it a free day to give me a shot at the board. Yeah, he definitely had. I wouldn't let him down.

Jada and Shayla ran to the first table. Their games seemed more fun than competitive, but Jada always won—she had game.

It was time to test my skills.

I took the empty spot playing against Lin. I had only seen Lin play one other time, and he wasn't that good—not that I was any better, but Lin had a relaxed mood that I kinda liked, and that seemed like a good first-time-playing-in-front-of-a-room-of-people vibe.

"Let's get started," Mr. Dennis called out.

This was it.

I chose the white pieces and took a moment to line

them up. When my pieces were all straight, I gave Mr. Dennis the nod—a move I'd copied from Twyla.

The game started just like I had practiced. My moves were slow and thoughtful, and even though I was a little shaky with everyone watching, my nerves faded each time I slid a piece across the board.

When we moved into the middle game, I was in control. I knew I had him.

Lin was just moving pieces back and forth with no strategy. He captured as many of my pieces as he could without even thinking about protecting his king. Big mistake—you always have to protect the king.

I couldn't tell when we moved into the endgame, but I knew I was getting closer and closer to that king. I saw my opportunity and went for it. "Checkmate," I called out.

"Good game," Lin said. Then he headed to an empty chair to watch the next round.

Winning in real life was not nearly as huge as it was in my head—there were no cheers, and no kings being smashed. Lin didn't even seem upset that he'd lost.

But when Twyla whispered, "Great job," my heart danced inside my chest, and I almost forgot how to talk. Even if it wasn't a big deal to anyone else, I'd done it! I'd had my first chess victory.

I was ready to take on whoever was next.

···

I don't know what I was thinking. I mean, I know I wanted to impress Twyla, but I should've known better.

After I beat Lin, I was supposed to be done for the day. But on free day, Mr. Dennis let anyone who wanted to challenge one of the upper-tier players get a chance to battle. That way, everyone got a chance to level up, he said.

I should've just taken my win and gone home. But when Mr. Dennis asked who wanted to battle Deuce, I couldn't help myself.

"I'll do it," my voice croaked out.

"You?" Deuce rolled his eyes.

"Yeah, me!"

"You ready to lose in front of everybody?" Deuce asked.

"What if *you* lose?" I asked, sticking my chest out.

"Set up the board. I'll even let you go first." His smirk was back.

I could feel Twyla staring a hole into the side of my face as I set the board up. I knew I should have just walked away, but Deuce did something to me.

I sat behind the white pieces and started with the same move I used in the game with Lin.

Deuce counterattacked right away.

Then I went to the next move I'd practiced.

Each time I slid a piece across the board, I felt Deuce's confidence rise—and mine fall. I'd just been riding the wave of victory, and now I was about to drown.

I never got control of my strategy. The game was over.

Deuce won, but even worse—I'd lost in front of Twyla.

CHAPTER TWENTY-TWO

The drive home was quieter than usual—for me, at least. Mr. Dennis congratulated me on my win, but I kept waiting for him to tell me how *un*logical I'd been for going up against Deuce. He never did. But even if Mr. Dennis didn't tell me, I knew it hadn't been smart. I'd let one little win go to my head.

I decided I wouldn't bring it up.

On Mondays, we usually ate any leftovers from Sunday dinner with rice or beans added to it. Since we'd eaten beef stew for dinner last night, I figured we'd have more of that over rice, but when I stepped onto the front porch, the smell of frying chicken kissed my nose.

The heat escaping from the kitchen met me at the door. But I'd trade extra heat any day for a piece of crispy fried chicken. Nik and the twins were glued to the TV, so I went into the kitchen to see if Granny needed help with anything.

She was humming and shaking seasonings into a plastic bag filled with flour.

"Anything I can do to help?" I asked Granny.

"No, but you can keep me company if you want." She put the chicken into the bag and shook.

I'd normally have gone to watch cartoons with the kids, but it seemed like Granny had gotten used to me being around. So I decided to stay in the sizzling heat of the kitchen to keep her company.

"I'm glad we're having fried chicken and not left-over beef stew," I said. "I mean, I like beef stew, but . . ."

"No need in taking it back. I spent a little extra on dinner tonight; I get tired of leftovers too." Granny shook off the loose flour before putting the chicken in the hot oil. It hissed.

"You do?"

"Mm-hmm."

"So why we eat the same thing all the time?"

I couldn't believe I'd let that come out of my mouth.

"We eat what we can afford. Tracey and your pop bought food out every night and got you children used to eating all fancy. That fast food cost too much, and it's no good for you anyway. I never ate away from home the way you kids do now. Besides, I spend the exact same thing every week at Piggly Wiggly, and that food lasts from one end of the week to the next."

The heat in the kitchen ticked up a few degrees when Granny started preaching. Sweat covered my face and dripped down my back. But something about Granny's sermons was a little less mean these days, so I let the sweat pour and kept my ears tuned in to her.

"I'm on a fixed income—that means you only spend what you got and no more. Somewhere along the way, y'all young people got that mixed up," Granny said. "The love of money is the root of all evil—the Bible says that."

I didn't know what young people she was talking about, but I said "Oh" anyway.

When the food was ready, I sat in the kitchen at the two-person table with Granny and stuffed my stomach with fried chicken, mashed potatoes, green beans, and homemade biscuits. Granny and I didn't do much talking while we ate, but she said a lot even when she wasn't speaking. I knew she'd spent extra on dinner tonight to make us feel better about Ma working so much.

And it felt good that Granny cared.

I'd gotten my first *W* at the board and had the best fried chicken in Larenville—I counted today as a win.

CHAPTER TWENTY-THREE

The next day, portal school took longer than normal, mostly because of my hate for commas. Well, maybe I don't hate them—I just get tripped up on when to use them, and I had to finish two whole worksheets on using commas to separate coordinate adjectives.

After my schoolwork was done, Mr. Dennis called me into his office. A sinking feeling formed deep in my gut. I'd never been in anyone's office for something good, so I was expecting the worst. The last time I'd been called into an office I was expelled, so I hoped I hadn't done anything to get kicked out of the center.

"Hey, Mr. Dennis, you need me?" I asked, my hands stuffed into my pockets.

"Yeah, give me a moment. I just need to print this out," he said.

The machine sound of his old printer tapped away while I wondered what I was in trouble for. Two pages, then three, then four filled the printer tray.

"For the past eight years, the Carver Recreation Center has entered two players into the junior chess tournament," Mr. Dennis said. "It's in Charlotte."

"In Charlotte?" I asked. *That's my city!*

"The winner earns a prize of one thousand dollars," Mr. Dennis went on. *That's more money than I'd ever know what to do with.* "I've been working with Twyla and Deuce this year, and they're more than ready to compete."

Oh wow, Twyla got in—of course she did.

"This year I'd like to bring along a third player if anyone shows some promise," Mr. Dennis said.

"You think maybe Jada or Lin could do it?" I asked. I wasn't sure about Lin, but Jada probably could.

"Or you. You have a lot of work to do, but I think you have some raw talent."

"Me?"

"Yes, you. I mean, unless you aren't up for it."

For some reason it took me a second to really hear what he'd said. *Talent.* He believed I had talent?

"I didn't say that—I just . . ."

"Well, you don't have to answer now. Plus, you'd have to work hard for the last spot. For right now, just hang these flyers up."

Me? In a chess tournament? A real tournament? In Charlotte?

I grabbed the flyers and got busy taping them up around the center.

Charlotte Classic: Junior Chess Tournament

Tournament open to junior
players of all skill levels

Time control—90 minutes plus
30-second increment per move

Top prize $1,000!

The tournament was at the end of June, which meant I had less than two months of practice time to get good enough for the third spot. I wasn't sure if I could do it. But if Mr. Dennis thought so, maybe I could.

I was jumpy to talk to Twyla about the tournament. I wondered if she had ever been, and if she'd ever been to Charlotte. And mostly I wondered if she thought I was good enough to join her and Deuce.

I popped in my earbuds and waited for the clock to tick to three p.m.

Pop's music thumped in my ears, bringing back thoughts of him. Would he think I was good enough for the chess competition? He probably wouldn't. Pop was bad at competition—likely something I had inherited from him.

I remembered this one time when I was in elementary school and we had a class spelling competition to pick who would represent our class in the school spelling bee. Ms. Walker, my language arts teacher, said all the students had to participate. She didn't have to ask me twice—I was a good speller. I breezed through the first three rounds, and then it was down to me and a kid named Yisen Langley. Yisen was smart, but I wasn't worried. The winner of our class bee would compete against the other fourth- and fifth-grade winners.

Yisen and I sat side by side, waiting for the next word to be called. When it was my turn, I stood tall, thinking I'd been given the easiest word—*annoy*. I spoke easy and clear and spelled out *A-N-O-Y*. I heard a small snicker escape Yisen's lips. I had forgotten the second *N*.

Yisen spelled *recommend* with no problem.

That night at home, I'd told Pop about the word I missed. He insisted that *annoy* was a trick word. He even called the school to talk to Ms. Walker—which I knew wouldn't end well. I wasn't sure what he'd said, but the next day Ms. Walker reminded the class that losing gracefully was just as important as winning. She might as well have said my name aloud to the class, because all I heard was *Lawrence is a poor loser.*

The kids started piling into the center. I immediately went to find Twyla.

She and Kendra were dressed alike again, wearing purple crop tops and jean skirts. When they walked toward me, I saw a peek of Twyla's stomach.

"Dang, your belly button looks like a dirty raisin," Deuce called out from across the room.

He was talking to Twyla.

"You wanna start with me?" Twyla gave him a side-eye. "Let's talk about the F you got on your research paper. Yeah, the F you're hiding from Junior. The same F you had a chance to do over but you were too lazy."

The whole gym erupted in laughter.

"Man, whatever." Deuce waved a weak hand at Twyla.

"Yeah, that's what I thought." Twyla rolled her eyes in his direction.

That had to sting. Deuce just got roasted in front of the whole center. I was almost scared to say anything to Twyla after that rip. I was happy I didn't have any Fs she knew about.

"Hey, Twyla," I said, walking over to her.

"Hi, Lawrence. Did you put up the flyers about the junior chess tournament?"

"Yeah, I did. I was actually going to ask you about it."

"What about it?"

"Have you been before?"

"Nah, this will be my first time. Mr. D talked to me and my mom about it last week. My mom said I can go as long as my grades are straight As at the end of the year."

"Oh, you think you can do that?"

"That's no problem—I always get straight As. My mom don't play!"

I was impressed. She was smart and could rip better than any boy I'd ever met.

"So, it's you and Deuce, right?" I asked.

"For now, but Deuce ain't going nowhere if Junior finds out about his F!"

She said "F" extra loud to make sure Deuce heard her. But he was way on the other end of the court, probably cracking jokes on somebody else, trying to take the heat off him for getting roasted.

"Anyway, why you asking all these questions about the tournament? You wanna go?" she asked.

"Well . . . I was thinking . . . I mean, Mr. Dennis said maybe . . ." I could tell by the confused look Twyla tossed at me that I wasn't making any sense. "Mr. Dennis said the third spot is still open. I know I'll have to work real hard, but I'd like that spot," I finally spat out.

Twyla gave me an up-down look like she was a coach trying to see if I measured up. "Hmm, well, you have time to get good enough. You'll have to practice like every day, but it can happen."

"You think so?" I couldn't believe this could really be a thing . . . for me.

"Yeah. You need to start playing with me and Deuce—we're the best."

"I know. I just got beat by Deuce yesterday, re-member?"

"Yep, I remember. It wasn't that bad, really." Twyla smiled. "You'll have to get a chess set and practice at home. And there's this book in the chess room, *The Skill of a Chess Champion*—I learned a lot from it. You should check it out."

Reading a book about chess sounded kinda, well . . . intimidating. But instead of saying that to Twyla, I just nodded.

"If you do all that, you *could* be good enough for the third spot," she said.

"Okay, I can do that," I said. I only believed it a little. I mean, Ma had just started her new job and Granny barely had money to feed Nik, the twins, and me—there was no way I was asking for something extra. Where was I going to get a chess set from?

• • •

Twyla's words replayed over and over in my head. That had become pretty normal, but this time I was think-ing less about her cool voice and more about the fact that she thought I could be good enough to play in the tournament. I wasn't used to people thinking I could do good things. With her and Mr. Dennis believing in me, I had to give it my best shot. But first, I had to get a chess set.

After my chores were done, I asked Mr. Dennis if he had an extra board I could use. He pointed me to a dusty closet in the back corner of his office. It was filled with busted tennis rackets, deflated basketballs, and even a pair of dirty sneakers. Way on the bottom shelf under some old books was a wooden chessboard. In a plastic bag taped to the back of it were the chess pieces. Some of them were faded and chipped, but it looked like they were all there.

"That board is yours, under two conditions," Mr. Dennis said.

"Okay," I agreed without even knowing what I was agreeing to.

"One, you clean out that closet from top to bottom. Two, you commit to practicing chess every day. That's the only way you'll get better. Deal?" Mr. Dennis reached his hand toward me.

"Deal!" I said, shaking his hand.

I had my very own chess set. I would have cleaned the whole office for it—cleaning the closet was nothing.

While I was separating the trash from the maybe

trash in the closet, Junior came into the office and closed the door.

"You and I have a problem," Junior said.

"We do?" Junior wasn't the serious type, nothing like Mr. Dennis, so I couldn't imagine what was up.

"Yes, we do," he said. "I want you and Deuce to go to that tournament in Charlotte. Problem is, Deuce won't be going anywhere if he can't learn to focus on school, *and* it seems you need some extra chess practice, right?"

"Um, yeah."

"I have a solution—you in?" Junior asked.

I was smart enough not to agree this time without knowing all the details, so I just shrugged.

"Here's the plan," Junior started. "Deuce is banned from the basketball court until he gets his grades up; with all the mess he's been hiding from me, that will take until the end of the school year. He'll be doing extra assignments under my watchful eye at home."

That didn't sound like fun.

Junior continued. "And since he has to be at the center with me anyway and he can't play ball, he can practice chess with you after school instead."

Junior can't be serious! There was no way me and Deuce could practice chess *together*. Our fight hadn't been that long ago, and even if no one was still talking about it, I remembered.

"Is he going to be cool with that?" I asked.

"Is he?" Junior laughed, flashing his gold tooth. "He doesn't have a say-so. Now, are you in?"

I was pretty sure I didn't have a say-so either, so I nodded.

Junior walked away, leaving me in the junky office. I couldn't believe Deuce was going to be my chess partner.

I had just made a deal to play with my worst enemy.

CHAPTER TWENTY-FOUR

After dinner that night, I escaped to Ma's room with the book Twyla had told me about, my new chessboard, and a soapy cloth. The board was old and dusty—but it was mine. I laid out all the pieces on the floor and carefully rubbed each one clean.

When I was finished, I set each black or white—more like tan than white—piece on its square and tested it out. The board was a little beat-up, and some of the paint on the black squares had rubbed off, but that didn't matter. I'd worked for it.

• • •

My first chess session with Deuce the next day was pretty much a bust. I sat at the table in the chess room practicing moves by myself, and Deuce sat on the other side of the room, watching the clock. He stared at it so long, almost like he was trying to move time with his eyes. It didn't work, because five p.m. wasn't coming any faster. Every time I looked his way, he gave me the mean face and turned back to the clock.

This was a horrible idea.

There was no way me and Deuce would get along good enough to be chess partners.

I'd had my fair share of forced friendships—not that me and Deuce would ever be friends—but this was rough, like first-day-at-a-new-school rough. Like when-I-don't-comb-my-hair-for-a-week rough. Like the-third-Wednesday-I-had-to-eat-salmon-patties-at-Granny's-house-and-they-were-overcooked-so-they-tasted-like-dry-cardboard rough.

When I had beaten myself for the fifth time, I finally turned to Deuce and said, "So you gonna make me play myself all day?"

"I ain't making you do nothing!"

He had the same slumped-low-in-the-seat look I'd had when I was outside Mr. Spacey's office, waiting for Ma to come pick me up.

"Junior said we have to work together."

"Well, he ain't here, is he?" Deuce said, sending eye missiles across the room at me.

"All right, whatever . . ." I shrugged and got back to beating myself in chess.

At exactly five p.m., Deuce jumped up from his seat, leaving me to put away the chessboard and clean up.

If things kept going like this, I'd never get good enough for the tournament, and I needed to get in.

I didn't even know exactly when the tournament had become that important to me, but it was now. It was the only way I could get to Charlotte *and* get close to Twyla. And if chess was for thinkers, me being in an actual tournament would let her know I could think about something more than fighting.

Maybe I could strike a deal with Deuce, something that would make him interested in helping me get better.

How could I get someone who hated me to help me?

The best way to make a deal with someone is to find out what they need. "People will always prioritize their needs," Pop used to say all the time. Especially when he was looking to make some money. He'd go around our old neighborhood in Charlotte looking to fix someone's lawn mower or someone's car or someone's *any*thing. Pop was real good at convincing people they needed his help, and they usually did, because he could fix anything.

I wished Pop was here to help me now.

My problem was, I knew nothing about Deuce—just

that Mr. Dennis had said we had something in common, whatever that meant.

• • •

"What's up with Deuce?" I asked Mr. Dennis.

"What do you mean, what's up with Deuce?" Mr. Dennis asked, not answering the question. We were on our way back to his house from the rec center that afternoon. He was in his happy place, driving with one arm all the way out the window, his head forward, and his eyes glued to the road in front of us.

"We're supposed to work together, and he won't help me," I said. "He hates me."

"He doesn't hate you," Mr. Dennis said. "He *is* you."

"What does that mean?"

"It means stop asking me all these questions and talk to Deuce."

• • •

The next afternoon, I decided to confront Deuce straight up.

I filled my chest with air and waited for him. "What's up with you?" I asked when he walked into the chess room.

"Who you talking to?" he asked, glaring at me as he strutted by on his way to the other side of the room.

I'm talking to you, I wanted to say, but I swallowed those words. I needed his help. "I'm just saying, why you so mean to me? What did I do to you?"

"You didn't do nothing—you just here. And I don't like you." His words dripped slow and cold like water off ice.

"Look, I'm just trying to be nice."

"I don't need you to be nice."

He was making this so much harder than it had to be.

"But you do need me to keep you out of trouble with Junior so you can get back to the basketball court. And Junior said that wasn't happening until—"

"I don't need you to tell me nothing about what my dad said!"

And with that I shut up. I'd have to get to Deuce another way.

Instead of wasting the rest of the afternoon staring at the back of Deuce's head, I left the thickness of the chess room and joined the other kids in the open room. Lin was leading a game of dodgeball on the basketball court. All the younger kids rushed to the edge of the court, their legs nervy, their eyes wide and fixed on Lin. They were terrified and excited at the same time. I used to love dodgeball. I mean, what could be better than having a ball flying full speed at your chest? Or, better, your head? And then ducking to avoid it and hearing it smack against someone else's flesh behind you.

Dodgeball was a little like chess. Not that you'd get smacked with a ball, but there was the same nervous energy when you were waiting for your opponent's next move. Taking your eye off the ball, or the board, for even one second could get you tagged out or scrambling, trying to figure out what to do next.

After watching three kids get knocked out of the game, I spotted Twyla and Kendra in the corner sitting by the Ping-Pong table. They were polishing their nails and laughing at the kids being thumped with the ball.

"You gave up, didn't you?" Kendra asked when she saw me walking toward them. "But you did last longer than I thought." She waved her wet fingernails in the air and shook her head at me.

"I haven't given up," I said. "Not yet, anyway."

"I thought y'all had a deal. You can't let him mess up your chances of getting into the tournament," Twyla said. "And trust me, he'd rather be socking kids with that ball than stuck in the chess room with you. You need to find a way to connect with him—get to know him."

"How?" I asked.

"Right, how?" Kendra said, looking at Twyla with

the same confused face I had. "I've known Deuce since Mr. Funderburk's second-grade class, and I still don't feel like I *know* him."

"All I'm saying is, he isn't that bad. Maybe y'all like some of the same stuff," Twyla said.

"Well, he does like music, almost as much as he likes basketball," Kendra said. "He and Lin had a rap group in fifth grade, called Deuces. They even performed a song in the talent show that year. It was a disaster—Lin forgot his verse halfway in and Deuce had to freestyle a whole nother verse so they wouldn't get booed off the stage."

"For real? Deuces?" I laughed. That name was a sign of failure from the start, but maybe I could use music to get Deuce over to my side, or at least to get him to talk to me.

• • •

The next day in the chess room, instead of setting up the chessboard, I cranked up Pop's iPod loud, filled my head with Pop's music, and waited by the door for Deuce to come sulking his way to the room. Just like clockwork, he moped in at three p.m. And, just like I'd expected, he said, "What are you always listening to?"

It was working.

"Why do you care?"

"If you're playing it on that beat-up iPod, it must be some old-school stuff."

"My pop calls it classic—funk and hip-hop melted together. He used to listen to it all the time." I popped out an earbud and offered it to Deuce.

I was surprised that Deuce accepted it instead of shooing me away.

I couldn't tell if he was into it or if maybe he'd rather hear *some* music than no music. But when Pop's favorite song started to blast into our ears, Deuce smiled a bit and finally said, "This actually isn't too bad. I mean, I don't know what they're talking about, but the beat is dope."

"My favorite part is when the choir starts singing," I said. That part was like licking off the chocolate layers of a Reese's cup, waiting for the first taste of peanut butter.

When the choir sang out, Deuce got his taste. He rocked a little and hummed the words like it was something he'd heard before.

The music surrounded us as I let the playlist spin twice, back-to-back. Deuce was feeling it—almost like a freestyle was sitting right on his tongue.

And even though Deuce seemed to be in his own world and I was in mine, we didn't feel so far apart. The last song was ending when Deuce asked, "Where's your pop?"

"Huh?" I asked. A sour taste formed in the back of my throat. That question had come out of nowhere.

Deuce turned to face me. "Your pop, where is he? You said your pop *used* to listen to these guys. That means he don't listen no more, right? Where is he?"

"Uh, he's gone . . . for a while," I said, real quiet. So quiet I wasn't sure Deuce even heard me.

"Oh, okay," Deuce said, which made me think he knew what *gone* meant.

CHAPTER TWENTY-FIVE

Friday night—spaghetti night at Granny's house, which was starting to feel more like my house, too. I loaded my plate with noodles and meat sauce and joined Nikko on the blanket in front of the TV. I was looking forward to spaghetti night without Iris and Ivy. Aunt Carmen had picked them up straight from school again.

Between slurps of pasta, I heard that Nikko had gotten an A on her spelling test, that she and Cassy had learned a new dance, something called the Sham, and that she had a special assignment due next week . . . something about a historical figure. I have to admit I wasn't paying much attention to Nikko's rambling, but when she said she'd chosen Booker T. Washington as her historical figure, my ears perked up.

"There's a whole school in Larenville named after him, right?" Nikko asked.

"Yep, and it's a good school too." I figured now was a good time to talk it up. Not that I was in school or anything, but maybe next year I could get away from Andrew Jackson and Principal Spacey.

"Boy, what you know about the Booker T. school?" Granny called from the kitchen.

"I know all the kids at the rec center go there."

"That's 'cause they're too far outside of town to get into Andrew Jackson," Granny said, joining us in the living room.

"Mr. Dennis said the teachers at Booker T. are more like us and we can learn better from them." I couldn't remember exactly what Mr. Dennis had said that first day I went knocking on his front door, but he had said *something* like that.

Granny laughed to herself a little and said, "Well, it sounds like Dennis needs to do some reading. We fought for Black kids to go to school with white kids. Why in the world would we give that chance up?"

I didn't have an answer for that—maybe *I* needed to do some reading—but I did know I'd rather be at school with Twyla, Kendra, Lin, and even Deuce than getting into fights for the rest of my life at Andrew Jackson.

"Andrew Jackson is a good school," Granny added under her breath.

Good for some, I wanted to say, but I wasn't going to start a fight with Granny.

• • •

Ma had been working nights for a couple of weeks now, and I'd gotten used to sleeping in her bed. When I climbed in, my body fell into the perfect spot with hardly any twisting and turning. Some nights I lay awake, staring into the darkness, my mind swimming with thoughts of life before we came to Larenville. I could remember little bits of time from before Nik was born. But mostly I remembered when Nik was still a baby.

Ma, Pop, and me were so close then—glued together. My favorite thing about those days was story time. We'd all cuddle up in their big bed for a bedtime story before they sent me to my room for the night.

Every night Pop told a different story about some adventure he and Ma had been on or some cool place they'd visited. I knew most of the stories weren't true, but I didn't mind. Pop had the happiest smile when we were crowded up together, me and Ma listening to his made-up tales.

My favorite was the story of how Pop won tickets to see an NBA basketball game at the Charlotte Hornets arena. Pop was called to the court at halftime to make a shot for some huge prize. Out of all the people chosen, Pop was the only one to make the three-point shot. Two reasons I know the story wasn't true: (1) Pop didn't like sports, and especially not basketball, and (2) no matter how many times I asked him, he never told what prize he'd won. If I had won some huge prize, I'd definitely be telling everyone.

Then, when Nikko got a little older, things changed. Ma got busier. Pop came home less. And the stories stopped. I hoped with all my might that things would be normal again, that we'd all cram into the big bed and listen to Pop's voice and see his smile—but that never happened. That was when I figured out that normal was something made-up, just as fake as Pop's stories about his and Ma's wild adventures. Normal wasn't real.

On some of those nights when I lay awake in Ma's bed, I tried to remember the deep sound of Pop's laugh. I remembered him laughing—the look of it, the way his mouth opened wide and the wrinkle lines that streaked his face. But for some reason I couldn't hear the sound. It had been too long, I guess, and no matter how hard I tried, I couldn't make it form.

CHAPTER TWENTY-SIX

Monday was chess-tournament day at the rec center, and my stomach was flopping all around. I was supposed to be improving, but being forced into the chess room with Deuce wasn't helping me get any better.

I had been reading—trying to read—the book Twyla had told me about. The parts I could follow were good, and it had lots of pictures and a list of how even a beginner could beat anybody at chess, and it showed a bunch of different checkmates. I bet Twyla got a lot of her winning patterns from that book—which would explain how she was so much better than the rest of us.

After school, the kids all crowded into the chess room. And even though it was fun to watch the other kids play, I just wasn't feeling it. I silently hoped Mr. Dennis would ask me to sweep the lunchroom—anything so I could skip out on the tournament today. But of course that didn't happen.

Before I could settle into my spot in the corner, he called me over to the table to play.

I was going up against Lin. I was pretty sure I could beat him again. But what if he'd somehow gotten better and I'd gotten worse?

I knew I wanted to win more than he did. I'd have to prove it . . . in front of the whole room. The floppiness in my stomach was back, and there was no sign it was leaving.

If Junior and Mr. Dennis saw I hadn't gotten any better since last week, they'd never consider me for the tournament. Maybe that was what had my insides fighting me—I was straight-up scared.

Lin chose the white pieces, and I slid in behind the black pieces on my side of the board. I took a deep breath and willed my stomach to chill out.

There was this part of Twyla's book that talked about tempo being one move. The book almost made chess sound like music, in a way. It reminded me of how each beat came together to make up a whole song. I needed to make a move—but I also needed to create the tempo for this game and play to my own beat.

And then something clicked and it felt like I had

Pop's music giving me energy. I imagined the choir was singing for me, cheering me on. The music played in my head—slow at first, and then the sharp, punchy voices sang out over that thumping beat. That was just what I needed.

Lin made his first move. So did I. His second move was expected. So was mine. On his third move, one of his pawns captured one of my pawns. It was on. I leaned in close to the board and tried to slow down my nerves.

The choir slowed down too, almost like they were standing over my shoulder, watching my next play.

This move was pivotal, kinda like getting three red pieces stacked on top of each other in Connect Four. I needed to get serious. I pictured my queen marching across the board to the choir's rhythm. Sharp. Strong. Steady.

I took Mr. Dennis's advice and looked at the whole board before making a move. I tried to play out how Lin would counter before I moved each piece. I could move my king's pawn two spaces forward. But then what if Lin got his king's bishop out early? That wouldn't work. I needed to move my pawns toward the center of the board. That was the strategy.

I beat Lin in twenty-nine moves. Two more moves than it should have taken, but my stomach had calmed down and my fingers felt lighter. And without me even knowing it, the choir had helped me keep my head in the game.

• • •

Next I had to play Jada. I didn't think she'd ever beaten Deuce or Twyla, but she was good enough to go up against them. As far as I could tell, she was my competition for the third spot to the tournament in Charlotte.

Jada laid her rainbow notebook on the table and turned to a blank page. She picked the white pieces and made her first move swift and clean. Then, just as swiftly, she scribbled in her notebook—Mr. Dennis had rubbed off on her.

I took a deep breath, leaned in, and thought about my first play. Every play added a new rhythm to the match; I just needed to set the right tone from the very first move.

I'd found my tempo, and the choir was back. A little softer this time, but their voices were still ringing right on beat. I could almost hear Pop's voice humming along with them.

A forced puff of air escaped Jada's lips, but I kept my eyes down while I made my plan. All the scared had disappeared out of my body. I had the board in front of me and the beat around me. I couldn't remember ever feeling like I could totally control something before, but I had this. It was even better than dodgeball.

A laser focus came over me, and no matter what Jada did, I was ready. I beat her in thirty-two moves. Not exactly an easy win, but I was starting to feel like I really had a chance at that third spot.

CHAPTER TWENTY-SEVEN

When I'm old enough to drive, I want my own truck. The way I see it, a truck is a perfect vehicle. Tall enough to see over all the traffic, and big enough to fit whatever you need to in the back of it. Except mine wouldn't be as beat-up as Mr. Dennis's or as junky as Pop's.

I was thinking about what color my truck would be—red, definitely red—when the edge of the Ping-Pong table stabbed my leg. I was smashed against the right side of Old Blue's flatbed while Lin was smashed against the left side.

"You good?" Lin asked. I nodded. But I wasn't good. I'd picked the wrong side to sit on.

As soon as the bus had stopped outside the rec that afternoon, Mr. Dennis had called me and Lin over to Old Blue. He needed help picking up supplies—

some new balls and, more importantly, a new Ping-Pong table. Someone had accidentally bumped (gotten pushed) into one of the old ones, and there was a dent the size of a butt right in the center of it.

Junior said Lin and I would hold the new table down in the back of the truck "just in case the ropes let loose."

So there I was, holding the table down while also pushing it away from my leg and at the same time trying not to die from the heat beating down on my head. It had gotten hotter in just a week's time. And the sun definitely was more brutal here than in Charlotte. Ma called it country heat. I called it extra hot.

"Y'all okay?" Mr. Dennis asked from the driver's seat. I couldn't see him past the body bag of balls leaning against the back window.

"Yeah," I croaked out. What I wanted to say was *No, no—I'm not okay.*

"Wanna switch?" Lin asked.

Yes, thank you, God. "If you want to . . ."

So the next time Mr. Dennis slowed Old Blue down enough that we could stand, Lin took my spot and I took his. The view was better (I could at least see inside the cab), there was no leg stabbing, and even the sun was less beaming.

Riding in the back of a truck in Charlotte would get you pulled over by the police. It could also get you and the truck "searched on suspicion." And if you kept all kinds of junk stored in it, you'd get searched all the time. Just ask Pop.

Pop's truck was black, and even though it was kinda new, it was almost never clean. Since he went around the neighborhood fixing everybody's everything, he also carried tools and random junk, like washing-machine hoses and lawn-mower wheels.

When I rode shotgun, I was mostly embarrassed by the trash, but also always looking out for blue lights.

"You're getting good at chess," Lin said.

"You think so?" I asked, even though I knew it. I'd picked up another win at yesterday's tournament, and I was beating Junior pretty easy now. With Mr. Dennis coaching from the seat beside me, my game was getting tighter.

"Yeah. You trying to get to the tournament, right?"

It was the most important thing right now.

"Yeah, I guess . . . ," I said, trying to play it down.

"That spot is yours." Lin said it so easy, like all I had to do was want it and it was mine. I'd never gotten anything just like that—but that was how it seemed to be for some people.

"You don't want to go?"

"Nah, chess isn't my thing."

I didn't know what his thing was. He rapped with

the freestyle kids, but I couldn't tell if that was something he really liked.

"So, what is?"

Lin shrugged. "I dunno yet. Everything's my thing
until I figure it out."

That made sense, and I kinda liked that. Lin *did* do
everything, with everyone. He was free to do whatever.

CHAPTER TWENTY-EIGHT

The next afternoon, Deuce slammed his backpack down onto the floor of the chess room and slung himself into a chair in the corner. He didn't even look my way. Something was wrong, and this time it wasn't my fault.

"How was school?" I asked. Not exactly smooth, but I figured I'd try.

"School is school. Oh, wait, you wouldn't know. You don't go to school," Deuce snapped back.

"A'ight, I was just asking 'cause you look like you had a bad day," I said. That didn't come out exactly right, but at least Deuce didn't snap back at me. He didn't say anything else, either, so I decided to let Pop's music fill the space between us.

I pressed play and handed Deuce an earbud. One, two, three . . . and then we were off. Full speed on a roller coaster over low bass and fast lyrics, zooming across the beat.

Seconds later, things felt a little less stormy, and I thought I saw Deuce's shoulders relax a bit.

"He's upset, but he needs to understand this is what's best," a voice outside the chess room said. I turned down the volume.

Junior's voice was clearer as he got closer to the door. "He hasn't seen his mama in almost a year, and now he's refusing to even speak to her."

Deuce's shoulders tensed again.

"Is he talking about you?" I asked Deuce.

"What do you think?" He looked like a mix of sad and angry.

Then Junior appeared in the doorway. Instead of flashing me his gold tooth, he turned toward Deuce and said, "This isn't over."

"Why are you making me talk to her? She's not coming home yet!" Deuce's voice was loud and sharp.

"Watch yourself!" Junior said, raising his voice back.

That shut Deuce completely down. He slumped in his chair and crossed his arms over his chest. The room filled up with hot air as Junior glared at the top of Deuce's head. Junior stood in the doorway a couple more minutes, then stomped away.

"For real, you haven't seen your mom in a year?" I

asked after I was sure Junior was down the hall. It had been more than a year since I'd seen Pop. And even though lots of time had passed, I still remembered that ache in my stomach from when he first left.

"Yeah," Deuce said.

"Where's she been?"

"Gone."

And then I knew what we had in common.

• • •

The music took over, and for a little bit it felt like we weren't in some small town—we didn't have to worry about school and being in trouble or our parents being away. We just got sucked into the sound.

It's funny how music has the power to take you places. I'd never been to Atlanta, but I felt like I knew it. I knew its sound and vibe. I knew its energy. I bet Granny's hymns took her to church. Maybe even behind the pulpit. I wondered if her music gave her energy too.

When the clock ticked to five p.m., it was time for us to hop out the ride and walk back into the real world.

"Thanks for playing your pop's music for me," Deuce said on his way to the door. I kinda liked the way he said "your pop's music." It *was* Pop's music, and letting Deuce listen to it was like letting him meet Pop.

Sometimes I felt like Pop talked to me through the music. Not exact words, but more like a nod in one direction or another. Today felt like his way of telling me to keep trying to make things cool with Deuce.

Maybe it was working, 'cause Deuce didn't seem so tight when he walked out of the chess room.

• • •

I looked forward to the quiet ride home in Old Blue.

I leaned my arm out the window the same way I saw Mr. Dennis do every day. The hot almost-summer sun baked my arm, but I didn't move it.

We'd just pulled into his driveway when Mr. Dennis turned the engine off, took a long slow breath, and said, "Sometimes we go through things in life in order to pull someone else up with us."

I was pretty sure this was a listening conversation and not a talking one, so I just let those words linger in the truck awhile. After a few minutes, Mr. Dennis opened his door, rolled out, and said, "Tomorrow. Same time."

On my walk over to Granny's house, I thought about what Mr. Dennis had said and how he had pulled me along to the rec center with him. Was that what he meant? I might still have been wandering around downtown or walking on gravel roads with nowhere to go if he hadn't offered me a job. Which really wasn't a job, because I wasn't getting paid, but I had somewhere to be, and that was better than being alone.

CHAPTER TWENTY-NINE

"We're going grocery shopping," Nik said, running to meet me at the edge of Granny's yard.

"Why? Now?" I asked. Ma and Granny usually went grocery shopping on Saturday afternoons.

"Granny's gonna let us cook dinner."

"And why would we want to do that?" I asked. Cooking dinner sounded more like a punishment than a reward.

"I was telling her about Pop making Hamburger Helper and how he let us melt cheese on top," Nik said. "And I think she got tired of me asking, so she finally said we could try it here."

Hamburger Helper was literally the only thing Pop could cook. Oh, and eggs—he made all kinds of wacky things with eggs. My favorite was a hard scramble, when the egg got little brown crusted parts, with Spam and onions.

"Okay, well, I guess we're making dinner," I said. If Nik was happy about it, I could be too. Usually on Wednesdays we ate salmon patties, so I was definitely good with Hamburger Helper.

"Let's see what y'all come up with," Granny said.

Me, Granny, Nik, and the twins loaded into Granny's car and rode to Piggly Wiggly.

Granny didn't say much on the ride, just hummed with the gospel choir on the radio, and she seemed happy enough to let us have a turn at dinner. Or maybe she was actually getting used to having us around.

"So what are y'all making for dinner?" Ivy asked. Iris had just asked the same question less than five minutes before, and I'd told her to wait and see.

"Something our pop used to make." Nik was shining with pride.

"Something like what?" Iris asked.

"Yeah, like what?" Back to Ivy.

The Ping-Pong of questions wasn't going to stop unless I stopped it. "You'll both see what it is when it's time to eat. Okay?"

"Okaaaay," they sang together.

Granny said me and Nik could pick out any meal we wanted and handed me five dollars. I flipped the wrinkled five-dollar bill in my hands, hoping it would somehow multiply itself. We had to feed me, Nikko, Granny, Iris, and Ivy, and leave leftovers for Ma.

Nik and I walked the aisles, collecting the items for our meal, while Granny and the twins waited in the car. We'd gotten the cheese and the seasoning mix and were headed to the meat cooler when Twyla appeared from the potato chip aisle, walking toward us.

My stomach twisted and dropped.

Do I say something?

We were too close for me to hide, plus I was sure she'd seen me.

Hey, girl. No . . . maybe *Twyla, meet my sister, Nikko.*

The space between us was closing faster than a sliding door.

That's Lawrence from the rec, I saw her mouth to a lady who had to be her mother.

"Hey, Lawrence," she said when we met right in front of the cooler.

"Hey," I said, trying to sound normal.

"I was telling my mom that you go to the rec with us," Twyla said.

Her mom skipped right past *hey* and asked, "Are you a student at Booker T.?"

"Um," I whispered. I couldn't tell her I wasn't a student *anywhere*.

"Is this your sister?" Twyla interrupted.

"Yes, I'm Nikko, but Lawrence calls me Nik," said Nik.

"Hi, Nikko, I'm Twyla."

I couldn't tell if her mom was annoyed or bored, but whatever it was, I didn't want to stand around any longer to find out.

"Uh, we gotta go," I said.

"He means we're cooking dinner tonight and we need to hurry," Nik explained, trying to make me sound less nervy.

"We're in a hurry too," Twyla's mom said, turning to leave.

"See ya tomorrow." Twyla waved.

And then they were gone *and* I was pretty sure Twyla's mom wasn't feeling me.

"We need one pound of ground beef." Nik casually read from the box like we hadn't just been face to face with Twyla and her mom.

"Five dollars and seventy-two cents?" Nik asked under her breath when she lifted the beef from the cooler. "We don't have enough."

Hamburger Helper was out.

"We got this," I said, hoping to cheer Nik up, but after three laps around the store we were running out of options.

We finally settled on hot dogs, but with real hot

dog buns, not loaf bread. The hot dogs and buns took up the whole five dollars (four dollars and sixty-three cents, to be exact), and we had nothing left over for anything to add to it.

By the time we got back home, Iris and Ivy had already started their normal fighting.

"I'm hungry." That was Ivy. "Me too." That was Iris. "Can y'all really cook?" Ivy. "Yeah, can y'all reeeally cook?" Iris.

"Y'all just watch cartoons until we're done," I said.

This must have been why Granny started dinner before the kids were out of school. Trying to tame eight-year-olds was much easier when they weren't hungry. Granny was safely tucked away in her room while we got to work. Nik boiled the hot dogs and I went through the pantry trying to find something to put with them.

My choices were pork-and-beans, corn, peas, and mixed vegetables—the dented cans all stared at me from the second shelf of the cabinet. I grabbed the corn and mixed vegetables. Now I had to figure out how to open the cans without asking Granny for help. Back at home in Charlotte, we had an electric can opener that held the can in the air and spun it around, and voilà, the can was opened magically. Granny didn't have one of those.

She did have a handheld thing with a turning handle

that I'd seen her use. I'd never thought about how it worked, just knew that it somehow opened cans. This cooking thing was harder than it looked. After knocking, banging, hitting, and twirling the can eight times, I finally figured out that the handheld thingy had a blade—two blades, really. And if you placed the can just right, and twisted the handle, it was possible to open the can.

So, thirteen minutes after I'd decided on corn and mixed vegetables, the cans were open. I dumped each into its own pot and turned up the heat. I sprinkled them with salt and pepper just like I'd seen Granny do bunches of times, and before too much longer, dinner was ready.

"Smells like some real food is cooking in here." Granny sniffed, walking into the kitchen.

Nik and I stepped back, our chests poked out, proud of our first meal in Granny's kitchen. Our first meal in anyone's kitchen.

"Well, get the plates fixed and let's see how it tastes," Granny said.

I made Ma a plate, wrapped it in plastic wrap, and put it in the microwave.

Nik sat between the twins on the blanket in the living room while Granny and I sat across from each other at the small kitchen table. I scarfed down my two hot dogs before I even started on the corn and vegetables.

Granny did the opposite. She ate all her veggies be-fore she took a bite of her now-cold hot dog. I figured she must not like hot dogs at all and just ate it to make me and Nik feel good.

And, really, it did make me feel good. Not just be-cause we weren't eating salmon patties, but more because Granny had let us stand in her spot in the kitchen and do for her what she always did for us, and she didn't even complain.

CHAPTER THIRTY

"Are you ready for me yet?" Twyla asked the next afternoon.

I was in the chess room waiting for Deuce. I had our favorite song cued up and ready to go when I heard footsteps behind me. My chest pounded when I turned to see Twyla standing in the doorway instead of Deuce. I hoped she didn't want to talk about seeing me at Piggly Wiggly the day before.

"Ready?" I shrugged. Wait . . . was this about chess? I mean, I had been waiting all this time to sit across the table from her, but I definitely wasn't ready to play against her yet.

"Yes, ready? Are you ready? I've been watching you play. It's time to see if you are good enough for the third spot. Plus, it'll be fun beating you," she said with a little laugh.

I decided right then I would take this *L* any day if I got to play against her.

"Where's Deuce?" I asked after setting the board up.

"Not sure. He didn't come to school today." Twyla got comfortable in her spot behind the black pieces and gave me the nod to start the game.

I started with my signature opening. It had worked on Junior, but this was Twyla. Her counterattack was like a fort designed to hold me back. My middle game— if you could call it that—never came together. I captured a few of her pieces, but not because I was on my game. Really, nothing I did came out right. I never got into the rhythm of the match. Twyla beat me in nineteen moves.

"You treat your pawns like they're nothing," she said after the game was over.

"What do you mean? Pawns *are* there to get taken, right?"

"Pawns are protectors. Yes, they get taken, but they're there to protect the king and queen. Even the most powerful need help to win. Use your pawns to help them—don't waste them."

The way she talked about chess was so plain and easy to understand.

"How'd you learn all this stuff?" I asked. "I tried to read the book you told me about. . . ."

"What'd you think?" Her eyes lit up.

"It was fine—kinda felt like I was trying to read another language. I did like the part about tempo, and the checkmate list with pictures was dope," I said.

"I had to read it like five times for it to really make sense," Twyla said.

"Five times?" *That* was why she was running through the whole rec.

"Yeah. I have a lot of free time. My mom doesn't like me watching TV during the school week, so it's homework or chess after I get home." Twyla shrugged. "Anyway, keep practicing. You need to get some games in against Deuce, too."

On the ride home, I kept thinking about Deuce and why he hadn't come to the center. Junior had been there, acting like everything was just fine, but no Deuce. It wasn't like me and Deuce were friends or anything, but I was a little worried about him, since he'd been in such a bad mood the last time I saw him.

Deuce didn't come to the rec center the next day, either. I decided to ask Junior what was up.

"Junior, can I ask you a question?" I asked after I was done racking the balls.

"Sure can," he said.

"Is Deuce okay? He hasn't been at the rec, and we're supposed to be getting ready for the tournament."

"Deuce'll be just fine," Junior said. "He'll probably be back next week."

I wasn't sure I believed him, but there was nothing else I could do.

I decided to make us a playlist for when he did come back to the center. Even if he didn't talk to me much, he did at least listen to Pop's music.

On my way from Mr. Dennis's house, I saw Ma's car in the driveway.

"Ma's here?" I whispered to Nik when I got inside. I was happy to have Ma home during the day, but normally she should have left by now. Knowing she wasn't at work got me scared for a minute.

Nik nodded. "She's sleeping."

"Yeah, Granny told us to be quiet," Ivy added.

"No, she told *you* to be quiet." Iris stuck out her tongue at Ivy.

I headed straight to Ma's room. I hadn't seen Ma in a few days, and even Granny couldn't keep me from checking on her.

She was tucked under the covers but sat up when I opened the door.

"Hey, Ma." I moved into the room. "What're you doing here?"

"Excuse me?" Ma said. "Is that how you greet your mother?"

"My bad, Ma. Guess I'm not used to having you here during the day."

"Now that you've interrupted my nap . . . If you're

wondering, and I know you are, I switched off days with Stacy."

Good, that was a normal reason to be home, and now I didn't have to worry.

"How's the center?" Ma patted the spot next to her for me to sit. "You're all into this chess stuff, right?"

"Yeah, I like it. I'm getting good," I said. I thought about telling her I was almost good enough to beat out Jada for the third spot in the tournament or how sometimes I heard music during a match. But that'd sound too weird.

"How's the chicken plant?" I asked instead.

"How you think it is?" Ma grinned.

"At least you don't bring feathers home anymore."

"Your granny said if I brought one more feather in her house . . ." Ma's giggles stopped her from finishing her thought.

I busted out laughing, 'cause Granny made Ma change her clothes before coming home now. "You'd think Granny would be cool with feathers for as much chicken as we eat!"

"Hush before she hears you," Ma said, lowering her voice. "If I never eat another piece of chicken as long as I live, it'll be too soon."

I tried to keep my laugh inside.

"Why does Granny act like that?" I asked, so low that the words barely reached Ma's ears.

"Like what?"

Ma was going to make me say it.

"I don't know . . . like everything's so bad," I said.

Ma chewed her lip and let out a deep breath.

" 'People are trapped in history and history is trapped in them,' " Ma said. Before I could even ask what that meant, she added, "Your grandmother is so busy trying to make sure we don't have the past she did, she forgets about the now."

I got that. Granny had lived in Larenville her whole life. It wasn't *all* bad, especially now that I had the rec, but I thought about those Confederate flags flying all around, and I wondered how many times Granny had had to pray to make it home safe. I bet her life here hadn't been easy.

Maybe Granny's fussing was her way of trying to pull us up.

Me and Ma let the silence rest between us. It was good having her at home during the week. It'd been so long I'd almost forgotten what it was like to be here laughing the way we used to during one of Pop's made-up stories.

After a few minutes, I asked, "Ma, you ever miss Pop?"

I'd been wanting to ask her that for a long time, but I wasn't ready to hear her say she didn't.

Ma closed her eyes like she was teleporting to

Charlotte, back to life before we came to Larenville, before Pop left. I bet she was picturing him fixing the pipe under the kitchen sink—it was always leaking.

"Mm–hmm," she said finally.

"Me too," I said.

"I know it doesn't seem like it, but your pop loves you and Nikko more than life."

"So why doesn't he call?"

"It's complicated, Lawrence." *Complicated* was a word I understood. "Things haven't gone right for your pop in a long time. And when things are going bad all around you, sometimes it's hard to do the right thing."

I definitely knew what that felt like, and for some reason I thought about Deuce and how angry he'd been that day before he stopped coming to the rec.

"Your pop'll be gone for a while longer." She paused to make sure I understood.

I did.

"After he's back home, maybe he can get some things to go his way, and he'll come around," Ma said. "I've spent my fair share of time being mad at him myself. And I still am sometimes—but the truth is, I don't think he's all to blame."

"Then who is?" I asked. I didn't want to blame Pop, but how could I not?

Ma turned to look at me.

"You remember all the times you told me about kids picking on you at school? How you wanted to get away? How it wasn't your fault?"

I nodded. Ma knew I remembered, but I was kinda surprised she did.

"That's what it's been like for your pop. There've been times he did wrong, I'm not denying that—he's made some mistakes—but other times when he was in the wrong place at the wrong time, other times when the system kept him stuck in a pattern of wrong." Ma sighed deep. "So it's not all his fault."

I thought about feeling stuck—that was something I knew all about.

CHAPTER THIRTY-ONE

The next week passed—no Deuce. Lin said he'd come to school Tuesday and Wednesday, but he hadn't come to the rec at all.

Online portal school was going good for me. My ELA assignments were done in about thirty minutes now. I submitted my work on time (early for most assignments) and never had to deal with Billy or Mr. Spacey. It was actually better than good, and I kinda wished they had let me do it all along.

The Monday tournament got moved to Tuesday because of Memorial Day, and I'd beat Lin and Jada (again). I'd also been working on my game with Twyla. She beat me seventeen times. But I was getting a little more comfortable playing against her. I'd figured out how to be more focused and not get caught up staring at her the whole match.

There was this thing she did—she raised her eyebrow in the cutest way right before she moved a piece. For two days, the brow raise threw me off my game, but by Thursday I'd learned to not pay attention to it. I was starting to get my competition rhythm against her. When she slowed down the cadence of the match—which was her signature strategy—I slowed the beats in my mind.

Thursday's match was our longest. I was getting better. And I felt more in control.

Jada and Shayla practiced a couple of tables over from us. It was mostly them talking and whispering, but I got the feeling Jada was watching me too. You know that feeling of eyeballs on your neck, eyeballs that suddenly turn away when you look in their direction? That's what Jada was doing. Then when she walked over to where me and Twyla were sitting, I *knew* she'd been watching me.

"Ready for a rematch?" Jada asked. Her chess notebook dangled in her left hand as her eyes met mine. "Let's see who really deserves the third spot in the tournament."

She was serious. The edge in her voice shook me for a couple of seconds.

Before I could even answer, Twyla said, "He's ready."

I was more than ready, if Twyla said I was.

I reached my hand out to Jada. "For the third spot," I said. We shook and it was on.

She straightened her black pieces and got ready to play. Instead of planning out my first move, I took a deep breath and found my beat. It was low at first but got louder when I concentrated on it. When it was just right, I focused on the board and my opening move.

Other kids gathered to watch, but I blocked them out. It was the beat, the board, and me. I could hear Pop rhyming to his music—my music—way behind me. Like he was cheering me on from the back of the room.

I'd collected all of Jada's pawns, her rooks, and one of her knights.

The choir rang in.

Fewer and fewer pieces were left.

I was getting closer.

"Check," I said. The choir was loud now. "Checkmate."

"Good game," Jada said when she got up from her seat.

"Good game," I repeated.

That had been my *best* game. Every move was in sync with the beat.

A huge smile covered Twyla's face. "That was awesome!"

I deserved the third spot, *and* I'd earned it in front of Twyla.

CHAPTER THIRTY-TWO

On Friday, I was practicing alone when Kendra called me from the chess room into the open room. Twyla and Lin were huddled in a corner at the far end of the court, whispering.

"Come over here," Kendra said. "Twyla wants to ask you something."

My face got hot. Could this be it? Twyla was in love with me and wanted to make me her boyfriend.

"Lawrence, can you keep a secret?" Twyla asked when Kendra and I joined the huddle.

"Yes?" I answered, not sure what was going to happen next, but whatever it was, my answer would be yes.

"Deuce is sick," Twyla said. "Ms. Klein, our homeroom teacher, told us that he'd be out for a while."

"For real?" I asked. "What's wrong with him?"

"We don't know," Lin said. "But he got sick like this before when his mom—"

Kendra interrupted. "You know he don't like people talking about that."

"Did she come home?" I asked.

"You know about his mom?" Twyla asked.

"Not really . . . just that she's been gone awhile," I said. I wondered if I'd said too much. I was sure they knew more than I did, but Deuce had kinda shared it with me.

"Well, don't tell anyone else. Junior hasn't even talked about it, but we were thinking about going to see him after school on Monday." Twyla looked hard at me. "I know y'all aren't best friends or nothing, but I do think it'll be cool to let him know we miss him."

"Okay, I'm in. Just let me check with Mr. Dennis," I said.

"Good," Kendra said. "Me and Twyla will make sure it's okay with Junior, and we can meet here after school and walk to his house."

• • •

The whole weekend I thought about what could be wrong with Deuce. He didn't sound sick, not like with-a-cold sick. And Junior had said he'd be fine. If it had something to do with his mom being gone, maybe he had that same pain in his stomach I had when Pop left.

I'd missed a bunch of days from school then. Sometimes it felt like a heavy blanket was weighing me down and I didn't have enough strength to lift it. Ma was feeling pretty bad back then too. She slept a lot and watched TV when she wasn't sleeping. She'd send me and Nik to Zack's Hamburgers to get burgers and fries for dinner most nights. Back then, a cheeseburger with extra pickles gave me something to look forward to and made everything better.

If Deuce was that kind of sick, time was the only thing that could help. If I got the chance, maybe I'd tell him that.

CHAPTER THIRTY-THREE

Monday afternoon, I waited outside the rec for the bus to drop the kids off. Twyla, Kendra, and Lin got off last, and instead of going inside, we headed down the road toward Deuce's house. We'd gotten permission from Junior and Mr. Dennis to miss chess-tournament day, and Mr. Dennis had agreed to pick me up after he closed the center.

"Do y'all know what to say to him?" Lin asked.

"Just act normal," Twyla told us. "He's the same Deuce."

"Cool. Just asking," Lin said.

I was glad he'd asked, because I wasn't sure what to say either. "The same Deuce" sounded like that guy who stole my earbuds and teased Twyla about her belly button. Maybe that wasn't really who Deuce was, though. If Twyla thought we needed to skip the best day of the week at the rec to visit him, he must be better than what he'd shown me.

We walked a mile in country heat before we reached a small neighborhood of houses. It looked a lot more like a Charlotte neighborhood than Granny's street did. The houses were closer together, and some even had garages. Lin, Kendra, and Twyla all lived there—most of the other kids from the rec did too. Deuce's house was down one of the back streets. Twyla rang the doorbell.

Deuce swung the door open as soon as the bell went off.

"Y'all skipped tournament day?" he asked with a half smile.

"Yep, but don't get used to it," Twyla said.

Deuce moved backward inside the room so we could all come in.

"Junior didn't say everybody was coming."

"Just the best of us came," Kendra said.

"Ain't no best without me!" Deuce tapped his chest.

That made me laugh a little. Maybe he was the same Deuce after all.

"I thought you were really sick," Lin said. "This is just an act for you to get out of school, right?"

"The school falls for it every time." Deuce laughed.

"No, for real, how are you, though?" Twyla asked.

His smile turned flat. "Better than last week." Deuce

looked just fine on the outside; I figured maybe his insides were where the pain was.

I didn't exactly know if I was welcome, but since I was here now, I figured I better say something. "We thought you might want someone to come see you."

"Thanks." Deuce didn't look mad, but I couldn't tell what he was thinking about me being there. "And let me guess, Junior made you come along so I can keep schooling you in chess?"

"Nah, I wanted to come," I said. Besides, we'd only had one chess match against each other.

"He's getting really good," Twyla said. "I'm not saying he can beat you, but I *am* saying he's way better than he was. He just beat Jada again."

"Oh please, he ain't ready for me," Deuce said.

It felt good for Twyla to speak up for me and for Deuce to diss me. Well, not good to get dissed, but it made things feel less weird with him joking around.

We all sat down on the couch in the living room. Deuce pressed play on his tablet, and the YouTube video he was watching rolled. It looked like some kind of rap battle. A word appeared on the screen, and a group took turns spitting rhymes that included the word.

When *JUICE* appeared on the screen, Deuce paused the video and said, "Juicy Juice, mango, pineapple, grape—all kinds of juice, have you goin' ape."

Lin jumped in: "I got the juice to quench any thirst. The sweet stuff that make you wanna . . . curse?" That was *not* a bar.

Deuce shrugged and looked at me and then at Twyla.

Oh no . . . did he expect us all to battle too?

"I got the flavor. The hype. The flow. Bars dripping with juice. Ayyyy, you betta know." Twyla killed it! She was blessed with all the talent. Some people had it all. *Some people* was Twyla.

Kendra and I sat the battle out. No way could we follow Twyla.

Twyla, Lin, and Deuce battled back and forth till we were all laughing too loud to hear them. I couldn't remember the last time I'd had this much fun. Screaming out answers to *Jeopardy!* with Granny and Nik was okay, but this was real fun, with kids my own age.

When the battle was over, Deuce passed around Doritos and Gatorade. We cracked jokes and munched until we heard voices outside in the street. Parents must have picked up kids from the rec—that meant Mr. Dennis would be here soon.

"All right, Deuce, see you later." Kendra stood up. "I have to go home and help with dinner."

"Yeah, I got homework," Lin said. "I gotta go too."

The fun was over.

"Cool, thanks for stopping by," Deuce said. His

voice sounded about as dull as I felt. Not that I didn't want to go home . . . I just hadn't felt like this since we'd come from Charlotte.

Lin, Kendra, and Twyla moved toward the door.

"Is it okay if I wait here for Mr. Dennis?" I asked.

"Sure," Deuce said.

Then it was just Deuce and me. It had been just us in the chess room together, but this was different. This was Deuce's territory. He controlled this board.

It was quiet for a while before he spoke. "So everybody think something is wrong with me, right?"

"Nah, nothing like that," I said. "Hardly anyone even brought you up."

"Dang, y'all already forgot about me?"

"Everybody just doing their own thing, I guess. Plus, Junior hasn't said anything, so we didn't know if it was okay to ask any questions."

Deuce didn't respond, but he didn't stop me either, so I added, "Twyla put this whole visit together."

"So you came 'cause you wanted to hang with her?" he asked. Did he know I was feeling Twyla? Nah, I hadn't been acting thirsty or nothing.

"No, I came because I wanted to make sure you were good," I said.

"Yeah, right. After all the stuff I did to you?"

"I know we ain't friends or nothing, but we ain't enemies, right?"

Deuce laughed a little. Maybe I shouldn't have asked that. I wasn't sure I really wanted to know the answer. "No, we not enemies," he said. "My bad for making it seem like we were. I'm not good at meeting new people. I should've given you a chance, 'cause you aren't that bad."

If this was Deuce's version of an apology, I was happy to take it.

"We're good," I said. "Oh, I made us a new playlist. It's all old songs, but it's the best of everything on the iPod. It'll be ready for you when you get back to the rec."

"Okay." Deuce smiled.

"My pop used to say music is freedom," I said. "I don't know about *all* music, but his music does make me feel like I can go anywhere."

"I get that . . . ," Deuce started. He looked around the room. "That's how rapping makes me feel. Like I can say whatever I want and it'll be okay." Then he looked past me out the window and breathed deep. I waited to hear whatever Deuce was about to say next. "I . . . um . . . I'm seeing this counselor lady, and we talk about music sometimes."

"Oh . . . that sounds nice," I said. I really had no idea what to say, but it *did* sound nice to have someone to talk to about things.

"And she wants me to try to go back to school soon."

"You want to do that? Go back to school, I mean."

"Kinda. We only have a couple more weeks left, and she thinks I should be there to say goodbye to my friends and teachers. Junior said once I'm back at school, I can come back to the rec."

"We'll all be waiting for you," I said.

It was quiet while we watched for Mr. Dennis and Old Blue. It was a cool quiet, though, not at all like those first days in the chess room. I'd had a bunch of enemies and a few friends during all the times I'd moved around, so I knew the difference between them.

Maybe Deuce and I were becoming friends.

CHAPTER THIRTY-FOUR

That night in bed, I thought about Deuce missing so many days of school—not like I hadn't missed a lot myself, but Deuce seemed like the kind of person who needed to be around people all the time. If he was skipping out on school and the rec, he must really have a lot going on in his head crowding out the good thoughts.

I tried to pack stuff away into separate boxes in my mind, leaving space for the good things. Which wasn't exactly easy, and sometimes it didn't work at all.

And really, I don't know when I figured out how to do that—probably after moving all those times. No reason to carry around boxes of bad memories from place to place. I just pushed all the bad stuff into a box and left it behind.

Charlotte and Pop were packed in two different

boxes. I mostly thought about Charlotte as being a place I could get back to one day. I tried to think about Pop like he was on a long trip. Not sure when I'd see him again, but I was certain I would one day, and for now I had his music to remind me.

Maybe Deuce had done that with his mom. Maybe a long time ago he put her in a box and pushed her way in the back of his mind. Now she was here, pushing her way to the front, begging to get out of the box. That was enough to make anybody sick.

• • •

The next morning, Junior came to find me in the chess room.

"Last night Deuce was the happiest I've seen him since all this mess started," he said.

What mess? I wondered. But if he'd wanted to say, he would have.

"Ya know, Deuce is a strong kid, but even the strongest of us need a little time to be weak." He looked around a bit, then said, "I guess I'm trying to say thank you for cheering him up. I know you two didn't start off on the right foot."

Getting into a fight was definitely *not* the right foot, but things were better now.

"We wanted to make sure he was okay," I said.

"And don't tell him I mentioned his name and *weak* in the same sentence," Junior said as he headed toward the door.

· · ·

We were just weeks out from the tournament in Charlotte, and chess was all I could think about. Nik had even caught me playing air chess—moving my hands like I was competing in a real match—while we were watching TV. And with Deuce not feeling his best, I wondered if he was still good to go. Would we need a replacement for Deuce just in case he wasn't up to playing? Jada was the next best player behind me.

I must not have been the only one thinking about the tournament, because on the way home Mr. Dennis said, "We'll be ramping up to two tournament days a week from here on out. It's safe to say your spot is secured, but now you need to focus on beating Twyla to get better. Steel sharpens steel." We both knew I was never beating Twyla, but I got his point.

"What about Deuce?" I asked.

Mr. Dennis took a long, slow breath and said, "That's a decision for Junior and Deuce. I'll train whomever I can. My top three players will go."

I didn't like the idea of Deuce not being in the top three, but it felt awesome to be chosen. I'd had a lot of losses, but this was definitely a win.

• • •

Granny and I had just sat down at the kitchen table, leaned over our roasted chicken and rice, when I told her the good news. "Mr. Dennis said I'm good enough for a spot in the tournament in Charlotte. I can go, right?"

Granny didn't say anything at first, but just pressed her fork into her chicken. I didn't know what I was expecting her to say, but I *did* want her to say something.

"All that work paid off," she said finally. It really was more about what she didn't say. I'd learned how to read between Granny's words. The words she didn't say and the proud shine in her eyes were all I needed.

CHAPTER THIRTY-FIVE

I'd finally made it to the last day of school! Not that I had been *in school* in a while, but I'd submitted my last online assignment, and Ma had gotten a letter recommending that I be promoted to the eighth grade. Which meant I was actually a decent student, just like the rest of the kids at Andrew Jackson. I definitely didn't want to be like them—and I was glad I didn't have to see them on the last day—but now maybe people would stop bringing up me getting expelled. And see me as more than that.

I'd bet Deuce was feeling the same way. Lin said Deuce had been at school every day for the last week—his homeroom teacher had thrown him a welcome-back party, even though it was the end of the school year.

Today would be Deuce's first day back at the rec.

Now that it was summer break, the center would be full of kids at eight a.m.

Twyla, Lin, Kendra, and I had gone to see him again before he went back to school, and he'd cracked jokes the whole time. He was almost the old Deuce—in fact, he was a more chill version of the old Deuce. I actually kinda liked this version. I just hoped his chess skills were still top-notch, because we needed him at his best.

With school over, and with the tournament in Charlotte just twelve days away now, Mr. Dennis said the two-a-week practice tournaments would turn into three-a-week practices.

When everyone loaded into the chess room early that morning, Mr. Dennis was waiting for us. "Today we learn about the importance of time." He held up a small machine with two clocks on it. "This is a chess clock. All games at the tournament will be timed, so it's best you get used to how it works."

Just when I thought I knew what I was doing . . . something new I *didn't* know.

"How does it work?" Lin asked.

"It's pretty straightforward. There are two buttons here. When a person makes a move, they stop their clock and it starts the opponent's clock."

Mr. Dennis looked around to make sure we got it. I was pretty sure *no one* did.

"Got it?" Mr. Dennis asked. Everyone lied with their nods. "Good, let's test it out."

And the practice tournament got going.

Mr. Dennis wasted no time dumping Deuce back into the action. For his first turn, he was up against Jada. She gave him a pretty good run, but he beat her. His next match was against me. He was a step behind his normal game after his first move. Then, after I'd taken two of his pawns, frustration stared at me from his side of the board.

"Oh, you the man now?" His eyes glared in my direction.

Talking during the match was a mistake. I knew he knew that. He was trying to get me off my game. Instead of answering, I just smiled and made my next move. We were ten moves in when the room grew extra quiet. I was playing to my own rhythm, and Deuce didn't seem to be playing to any rhythm at all.

Everyone was leaned in, ready to see if Deuce would lose. I already knew the answer.

When you're on your game, it's like everything slows down and you hear the music just perfect. Like that match was made just for you and your song. I felt like that right then.

It was my song.

I hated to beat him on his first day back to the table, but I had to do it. And I'm not gonna lie—it felt good.

"Okay, you got me straight up," he said after the game was over. He was trying not to make it a big deal, but his eyes told the truth.

"I got lucky." I didn't want to be the reason Deuce was feeling low.

"Don't try to make him feel better," Twyla said. "He lost." Then she turned to Deuce. "Get back on your game. We need you."

When everyone had left for the day, Deuce and I hung around the chess room stacking chairs. Since he'd been gone, I'd actually missed the times it was just me and him alone avoiding each other's eyes, trying to ignore each other.

I pulled out Pop's iPod, passed Deuce an earbud, and pressed play. My playlist started with a banger. The words were super braggy, and the beat was a slow thump—it was old-school, but fresh. And after beating Deuce for the first time, it was the perfect vibe for how I felt. My confidence bounced around in my body to the beat.

"This slaps," Deuce said, bopping his head.

"For real, for real."

I could almost see Pop walking down our street vibing to it and nodding at me like he'd heard about my win. I couldn't wait to tell him about it one day.

"We could use this as our theme song at the tournament. You know, like when performers onstage have a song playing in the background?" Deuce asked. "This can be ours."

"That'd be cool. We just have to make sure Twyla is good with it."

"She'll do anything you ask," Deuce said. "I think she's really feeling you."

My mouth watered a little, like when something super sweet touches your tongue for the first time. Twyla was feeling me?

"Nah . . . ," I said, too afraid to agree.

"She defends you all the time. Twyla never capes for anybody like she does for you," Deuce said.

She *was* always on my side.

"You gonna ask her to be your girl?" Deuce smiled like he'd just come up with the best idea.

"Nah," I said again. Deuce might have been sure Twyla had a thing for me, but I wasn't.

• • •

Since school was out, Nik, Iris, and Ivy had set up a summer camp right on Granny's front porch. There was a full rotation of jump rope, hand-clapping games, and screechy, off-key singing. I bet Granny yelled, "Y'all quiet down," at least five times an hour.

I did think about asking Nik to come to the rec with me, but the instant picture of the twins singing all loud in Twyla's ear was too cringe—it made me keep my mouth shut. Especially since Twyla *might* be feeling me.

That night, after everyone was in bed, Nik peeked her head into Ma's room.

"You sleep?" she asked.

"Nope, what's up?"

"You been acting funny," she said. "Like at dinner, you was all daydreamy."

"My bad, Nik. Just thinking about the tournament."

I couldn't tell her I was wondering if I was about to have my first girlfriend.

"I wish I could go with you," she whispered.

"Me too. It'll be kinda like going home." I'd been trying not to talk about the tournament too much around Nik; I knew she'd want to come along, and it felt kinda weird being so happy about something she couldn't do with me.

Nik looked down at her feet. "That's not our home. This is. I don't think about Charlotte anymore," she said. She crossed her arms over her chest. I could tell she didn't mean it.

Seemed like Nik had figured out how to put things in separate boxes too.

CHAPTER THIRTY-SIX

Deuce was back and on his game at the chess table. He and I took turns beating each other for the rest of that week and the week after that. When we weren't playing chess, we were listening to music. We mostly vibed to Pop's music, but Deuce also let me listen to his music, and sometimes he broke out into a free-style.

> *Deuce and L checkin' in,*
> *go tell a friend.*
> *We run the boards and stay locked in,*
> *to the beats, the flow, the rec—*
> *we da best.*
> *Try us if you want,*
> *get sent back pawn-less.*

I can't lie—Deuce was nice with it. And he was for sure free, letting his words float over the beat.

Twyla and Kendra had started teasing us for having a bromance. I'd normally have let that kind of thing get me all mad and ready to fight, but for a couple of reasons, I didn't mind. For one, I couldn't imagine fighting Twyla. She was good at everything and would probably whip out some karate moves and chop me down. For two, I liked Deuce—something I hadn't thought would ever happen. Real *did* recognize real. Me and Deuce were more the same than different.

"I hope y'all are practicing for the tournament as much as you're listening to that music," Twyla said Thursday afternoon.

She just didn't know—it was all I could think about. The tournament and Charlotte. First it was a week away. Then it was just days away. And now it was here: we were leaving for Charlotte the next day, and the tournament was Saturday. I couldn't believe it was so close! My body was itchy with excitement.

"Don't worry," Deuce told her. "We'll be ready."

"If you say so, besties," Twyla said on her way out of the room.

"She's just jealous you're spending all your time with me," Deuce laughed.

"Don't start that." I rolled my eyes. I couldn't help but break out into a silly grin, though.

"You need to just do it," Deuce said. "It's time you manned up."

He said that like every day now—something about me being too scared to ask Twyla to be my girlfriend.

"Oh . . . I get it. . . . You're waiting until the day of the tournament to ask her, right?" He nodded. "That's a great plan. So when she wins the whole thing y'all can kiss in front of everybody?"

"All right, all right, you gotta chill." I threw my hand up like a stop sign. The truth was, I was too scared to ask Twyla about being my girl, and I wasn't getting all pumped up for either of us to win. Twyla was the best chess player I'd ever seen, but I knew better than to get amped for something—that was a quick way to get disappointed.

And then Mr. Dennis called everyone onto the court for final instructions before the tournament.

"Ms. Linda will be in charge of the center tomorrow, since me and Junior will be driving our team to the tournament," Mr. Dennis explained. "Twyla, Deuce, Lawrence, we'll meet here tomorrow at noon."

Twyla's mom was also riding down with us. *Great.* I was pretty sure she still hated me from that time at Piggly Wiggly.

• • •

I barely slept that night. I packed and repacked my bag three times. My body had an electric buzz all over it. I was happy to be going back to my city, but even happier to be a part of the chess team. Just three months ago I hadn't had any friends, and now I had Lin, Kendra, Deuce, and Twyla, and Mr. Dennis and Junior. I felt like I'd found my people.

• • •

The next morning Granny made me an extra-special breakfast while Ma got some sleep after her shift. Pancakes, baked apples, bacon, and cheese grits. Me and Nik ate in the kitchen while Granny repacked my bag. Iris and Ivy were happy and quiet for once. And really, Granny's cheese grits had that effect.

"Nothing in this bag is folded the right way," Granny fussed. I knew she was just saying that, though, because I'd folded and refolded my clothes at least four times. This seemed like a big deal to her. She was acting like she had the same electric buzz I did: she didn't sit down the whole morning.

"You think y'all will win?" Nik asked me.

"I'm just excited to go," I said. Winning would be great, but getting there was where my mind was.

"You're coming back, right?" Nik asked.

"Yeah, of course," I said. "I'll only be gone until tomorrow afternoon."

"Lawrence, come here a minute," Ma called from her room.

I found Ma half-asleep sitting up.

"I wish I could be there to see you do your thing," said Ma. "I'm proud of you."

"Thanks, Ma." I reached in to give her a hug. "I'll do my best."

"Carmen left this for you." Ma passed me a notebook.

It had CHAMPION in gold letters etched on the front. When I turned to the inside flap, I saw she'd written, *For my favorite nephew.* And even though I was her *only* nephew, I loved being her favorite.

I gave Nik an extra big hug before I left to meet Mr. Dennis in his driveway. Granny packed me some snacks and stuffed some money into my pocket. I knew Granny didn't have much, so it felt special that she gave me anything at all.

"Don't go up there acting like you don't have any home training," Granny said.

I grabbed my bag, added my notebook from Aunt Carmen, and put Pop's iPod and Twyla's earbuds in my pocket and headed Mr. Dennis's way. The electric buzz was back and crawling all over my body.

CHAPTER THIRTY-SEVEN

Junior and Deuce and Twyla and her mom were waiting in the parking lot of the rec with their overnight
bags when me and Mr. Dennis got there. Deuce was
acting as antsy as I felt. Even Twyla looked a little
amped up. Her mom was extra chill, but she did say
hello to me this time.

We all loaded into the van Junior had rented—
Twyla, Deuce, and I called the back seat, Mr. Dennis
rode shotgun, and Twyla's mom had the middle row
to herself.

"We'll be there in about three hours, before any
rush-hour traffic can slow us down," Junior said. "Here
are the rules of the van: No one sitting in the back of
the vehicle has any say-so on the music played. No
stops will be made—any extra time spent on the road
will cause us to run into traffic, and I don't do traffic. It

is fine to sleep, not fine to snore. If you snore, anything that happens to you is fair game."

Junior looked at us in the rearview mirror and flashed us the gold tooth with each rule. He could've told us to sit stiff like robots for the whole trip and I wouldn't have complained. This was the best day I'd had in like a really long time; nothing could make it bad.

As soon as we got on the highway, Twyla pulled out a book, and Deuce was already watching YouTube videos on his tablet. So I popped in my earbuds and cranked the music while I doodled in my new notebook and tried to keep my body still.

• • •

We rounded the exit from I-277 and headed right into downtown Charlotte. Junior said, "Wake up, everybody, we're here!"

I was already awake, but Deuce and Twyla sat up just in time to see the Bank of America Tower and the stadium where the Carolina Panthers play. We rode past the NASCAR Hall of Fame and then the Charlotte Convention Center, where the chess tournament would be the next day. It looked like a Jenga tower of glass squares.

We passed a group of people posing near a street

mural with BLACK LIVES MATTER painted in different-colored letters.

"You left all this to come to Larenville?" Deuce asked me.

"Yeah . . . ," I said. I wanted to say, *It wasn't my choice,* but it didn't matter why we had left Charlotte, just that I was back now.

• • •

Our hotel was nice. Like really nice. Not that I had a lot of hotels to compare it to, but I was impressed. We walked through the huge sliding doors and onto shiny marble tiles. There was a giant chandelier (it took up the whole room) that lit the path to welcome us.

The adults checked us in while Twyla, Deuce, and I were too busy staring at all the glossy stuff around us to move. There was a sign that pointed left for the fitness center, right to the outdoor patio, and down to the pool. I wanted to do it all. I wished I'd brought some swim trunks.

When Deuce finally snapped out of shock, he convinced Junior and Mr. Dennis to let me and him stay in a room together. I couldn't believe me and Deuce would have a whole room all to ourselves.

"Y'all have a couple hours to hang out before dinner," Junior told us.

"Don't leave the hotel," Mr. Dennis said. "Meet us in the lobby at six p.m."

"And don't do anything I wouldn't do," Junior said.

We had two whole hours to do whatever we wanted.

Deuce and I climbed into the elevator, pressed 7, and made it to our room.

First we stuffed our bags into the closet and picked our beds. I chose the bed closest to the window. Deuce removed the sign on his bed that told him he'd have the best night's sleep ever, kicked off his shoes, and climbed under the covers.

"Deuce, we have to see the rest of the hotel! We don't have much time," I said.

"I was trying to see if that sign was telling the truth," he said.

• • •

Deuce, Twyla, and I met up and roamed the whole hotel. We went back through the mile-tall lobby lit up with the monster chandelier, then checked out the outside pool, the inside pool, and the theater room.

There were free snacks in every room we went into. Fruit kebabs by the pools, pretzels in the lobby, and popcorn in the theater. We helped ourselves to some of each.

At the snack bar on the second floor, we grabbed some nuts and fancy water from a pitcher filled with lemons and limes, and then me and Deuce went back to our room to flip through channels on the TV before dinner, while Twyla went to get ready.

Soon Granny and Nik would be eating spaghetti and then watching *Jeopardy!* For a minute I wished Nik was here to see how cool all this was: Charlotte, the hotel, all the channels on the TV—even the snacks.

"When you gonna do it?" Deuce asked, pulling my thoughts away from Nik.

I searched my brain for something I was supposed to be doing.

"You scared?" he asked.

I really had no idea what he was talking about, but I wasn't scared of whatever it was. "Nah, I'm not scared."

"You gonna ask her tonight or tomorrow?" he asked, giving me a *dare you* smirk.

Oh, Twyla. There he went again with the Twyla-being-my-girl thing. It wasn't like I didn't want to ask her, I did . . . but, okay, maybe I was scared. I mean, she could say yes—that'd be great. But I'd have to act like a boyfriend, and I didn't know how a boyfriend was supposed to act. Or she could say no—that would be bad. Or she could say no *and* get mad at me for asking and not even want to be my friend anymore—that would be *the worst*.

"Uh, maybe tomorrow . . . ," I said.

"There'll be too much going on tomorrow with the tournament. You should do it tonight."

"You're the one who said I should do it the day of the tournament!" I said.

"I changed my mind. . . . Tonight is better. Do it tonight," Deuce said, like he could see into the future.

Deuce *could* be right; he'd known Twyla a lot longer than I had, and he'd probably had lots of girlfriends.

I flipped the channel on the TV and pushed the whole thing out of my mind.

· · ·

We met everyone downstairs at six p.m. and headed to dinner.

We pulled into the Pinky's parking lot ten minutes later. Pinky's had some of the best burgers in the city. It had been on the show *Diners, Drive-Ins and Dives,* and there was even a car on top of the restaurant. Yup, a whole car—it was small, what Pop called a "punch buggy," but it was still a whole car. Along with the best burgers, Pinky's also had the best fried pickles. It had been forever since I'd had some, and my mouth started watering as soon as we walked through the door.

"I'm getting the Mammoth burger," Deuce said, reading the menu. "And what are fried pickles?"

"You've never had fried pickles?" I asked. I'd never seen them in Larenville, but I'd figured that had a lot to do with Granny and her weekly menu of home-cooked meals.

"I don't like pickles . . . so why would I eat a greasy *fried* pickle?"

"They're fried, but they aren't greasy," I said. "Trust me, you'll like them."

"Cool. I'll have French fries *and* fried pickles, then," Deuce said to Junior.

"You're so greedy," Twyla said. "But if you get fried pickles, can I have one?" We all laughed.

"Get whatever y'all want. It's on me," Mr. Dennis said.

I got the Trash burger—a regular cheeseburger topped with fried pickles, onion rings, and a creamy ranch sauce. And I ordered a strawberry milkshake. Deuce and Twyla got milkshakes too, and we shared a basket of fries and a basket of fried pickles.

My burger was just as good as I'd remembered. Actually, it was better than I'd remembered—with the perfect amount of juice dripping onto the plate and cheese oozing out under the bun. I ate every single bite and almost licked my plate clean before I remembered I was eating at a restaurant, with Twyla watching.

CHAPTER THIRTY-EIGHT

When we got back to the hotel, Deuce begged to get one more practice in with Twyla before the tournament tomorrow. "Practice makes perfect, right?" he said to Junior. "And our team needs to all get on the same page."

He was setting me up, I knew it.

"One game out here in the lobby," Twyla's mom told us. "Then up to bed."

Twyla and I sat at a little table in the corner of the lobby while Deuce went to get a chessboard. Twyla was talking about how cool the city was and how she could eat a whole nother basket of fried pickles all by herself. Normally, I would have loved hanging with her, but all I could feel was a lump in my throat. The kind of lump that ate up any words trying to get around it. So I just nodded and kept my mouth shut.

When Deuce came back, he and Twyla played a quicker-than-normal game—well, quicker than *their* normal game. Twyla won, of course, and Deuce was starting to put away the chess pieces when he said, "Hey, Lawrence, why don't you walk Twyla to her room while I clean this up?"

That dang Deuce was putting me right on the spot. I tried to think of something smart to say, but that lump was back, chumping up any words that tried to get out.

"We better go—my mom will come looking for me soon," Twyla said. I somehow moved my legs enough to get up from the table and follow her to the elevator.

Twyla was talking about all the people who would be at the competition tomorrow when the door slid open in front of us. *At least it's empty.* She got on first and pushed the button for the seventh floor.

I have to do it now.

I swallowed hard, hoping to move the lump a little. *You can do this.*

"Um, Twyla," I said, my eyes glued to the floor.

"Yeah . . . ," she said.

"I was thinking, I mean, not really thinking. I was wondering . . ."

"Lawrence, you aren't making any sense," Twyla said. Her voice sounded worried or irritated; I couldn't tell which.

"I don't exactly know what a boyfriend does," I started again. "I've never been one, but I was hoping maybe I could be yours. . . ." The lump had dropped from my throat to my stomach in a quick thud.

Twyla's stretched-up eyebrows meant she was confused.

"I like you . . . ," Twyla said. "As a friend . . ." Some more words followed, but I couldn't make them out. I was mostly hoping this whole moment could just be over.

She was probably telling me how silly I was to think she wanted to be my girl.

CHAPTER THIRTY-NINE

When the elevator door opened, Twyla stepped out and said something that sounded like "See you tomorrow."

I didn't move. I couldn't move. When the door opened again, I was back in the lobby.

Deuce was there waiting. "So . . ."

My face was stuck in a flat frown.

Deuce tried again. "So, what'd she say?"

"I don't remember what she said, but she didn't say yes." I'd already forgotten what words she'd used, and even if I had remembered, I wasn't repeating the complete embarrassing play-by-play.

Deuce's face went from excited to surprised, then landed on something that looked like pity. "Oh . . . my bad." He elbow-bumped me and got in the elevator.

I have to give it to Deuce: on the way up he did try

to make me feel better. Saying that Twyla could still change her mind or I could try again after we were back in Larenville. But really, that just made me feel worse.

I collapsed on my bed, hoping sleep would come soon.

Here I was, back in Charlotte, in a hotel with my *own* bed, with someone I was finally friends with, and all I could think about was Ma's lumpy bed back at Granny's.

I should've known better than to step to Twyla like that. She was the smartest, prettiest girl I'd ever talked to—no way she'd want me as a boyfriend.

I'd just have to pack her no away in a box like all the other bad stuff that happened in my life. Which wouldn't be easy since I had to see Twyla at breakfast. *Ugh! I should've stayed in my lane.*

• • •

I woke up the next morning in a foggy cloud. I'd barely slept. Twyla's face kept appearing in my dreams. I thought about what I should say to her today. We'd be leaving for the convention center soon, and my mind wasn't on chess at all.

"I've got the perfect solution," Deuce said as he was

putting on his clothes. "Try to talk to another girl at the tournament."

"What?" I asked. That was a horrible idea. I was really starting to like Deuce—but man, he had bad ideas.

"It doesn't matter who it is. Just make sure Twyla sees you," he went on. "Girls get super jealous like that."

"Deuce, I'm done taking advice from you," I said. And I meant it. He was the one who got me all hyped in the first place. I needed to handle this my own way.

I was practicing what I wanted to say in my head when Twyla walked into the breakfast room at the hotel. Suddenly my cereal tasted like wet dirt and my throat got lumpy all over again. Me and Twyla were friends—I should have just kept it at that, but no, I'd gone and messed it up. This time there was no one to blame but me.

I avoided Twyla's eyes while she fixed her plate. I hurried to finish my breakfast and rushed outside to wait for everyone else. I knew I'd have to say something to her at some point, but I was going to avoid it as long as I could.

• • •

We walked down the block from our hotel to the convention center. The streets buzzed with noise and people. Not too many people that you would feel lost—just enough to feel little butterflies of energy flying around you.

"Junior, this might be the best thing you've ever done for me," Deuce said, looking up at the buildings surrounding us. "Oh, I forgot about the burger and fried pickles—this might be the second best thing you've ever done for me."

"You can pay me back by kicking butt today," Junior said.

"Y'all ready to compete?" Mr. Dennis asked.

I was dragging behind the rest of the group—trying to stay clear of Twyla.

A small wave of relief brushed over me when we reached the convention center. I stared up at the enormous angular building, made of a thousand glass windows. My fourth-grade class had come here for a concert once. I remembered feeling important, marching in with my friends back then—who'd have ever thought I'd be back here to compete?

A massive banner hung from the ceiling inside: CHARLOTTE CLASSIC: JUNIOR CHESS TOURNAMENT.

Just a couple of months ago, I got kicked out of school and was wandering around a town that didn't want me; now I was here in this fancy place with kids who'd probably been playing chess their whole lives.

It almost didn't even feel real. It reminded me of

a scene out of one of Pop's stories. I knew he'd have a funny story to tell about this place. But since this was really happening, I'd have my own story to tell him one day.

"Follow me to the table so we can sign in," Mr. Dennis said, directing us over to a long line.

We stood behind the line marked A–C, for Carver Recreation Center. There were a bunch of kids and parents looking for their line too. Most of the kids were white, with preppy haircuts and polo shirts and too-starched khakis.

Everyone was all intense-faced, like they were ready to battle. I'd never thought of chess as a sport—one that needed a uniform I wasn't wearing. I'd thought about it more as a game, something to take my mind off everything happening around me, but these kids looked serious. Maybe I was wrong to think I could really compete against them.

Suddenly I had the too-familiar feeling of trying to blend into an almost all-white space like at Andrew Jackson.

Junior must have noticed the drowning look on my face, because he grabbed my shoulder and said, "Don't let these kids intimidate you. You belong here just as much as they do."

• • •

After we signed in and got our name tags, Mr. Dennis called us over to a corner and showed us the tournament schedule.

Each player played one game at a time—one and out, or, like Pop used to say, win or go home. Mr. Dennis explained that at each level someone would be eliminated. The team with the last player standing would win a thousand dollars.

That could buy a whole lot of burgers, fried pickles, and milkshakes. Or take me, Nik, and Ma to Myrtle Beach for the weekend.

Then it was time to move into the tournament room.

It was bigger than I remembered from the concert. Rows and rows of chess tables filled half of it. Instead of the boards being wood, they were flat sheets of cloth, with blue or green squares. And there was a clock at each station—just like the one we'd practiced with. This was the real deal—the sweat gathering under my armpits told me so.

Deuce and Twyla looked just as stunned as I did. They'd been playing chess a lot longer than me, but this was their first real tournament too. And after this we'd all be getting our own chess rating.

"We got this," Deuce said. It was almost like he could feel my wet pits.

"You think so?" I asked. My hope was fading fast.

"We're here now." Twyla sounded a little less cool than usual. "I didn't come all this way to lose."

She didn't look right at me, but she was talking to me. Or at least she wasn't *not* talking to me. That was a good sign.

"Deuce, come out here a minute." Junior motioned for Deuce to go out in the hallway.

Just when things were starting to feel a little better between me and Twyla, Deuce had left me alone with her again. *Try to be cool.* A nervous tingle crept up my left arm. I crossed my arm in front of my chest, then behind my back, and then shoved my hand into my pocket. The tingle wasn't going away, and this cool act wasn't working.

Twyla saved me by walking away.

I was about to go check on Deuce when I heard his voice over all the loud whispers coming from the hallway.

"For real, Junior?" Deuce was yelling. "You thought I wanted to talk to her now?"

Oh no! What's going on?

"Calm down!" Junior's voice was a raised whisper.

I fast-walked out to the hall to find them. Deuce had jerked away from Junior and was headed toward the main doors. I raced to catch him.

"Deuce!" I shouted.

He was pushing through the doors when I finally caught up.

"Wait up," I called out when we were both outside.

"I don't want to talk about it!" Deuce didn't even turn around.

"You don't have to talk—just slow down." We were halfway down the block now, and I didn't want to go too far; the tournament was about to start, and Mr. Dennis would be mad if we were late.

When Deuce stopped walking, I could practically see steam rising from his body. His eyes were narrowed like darts—they weren't shooting at me this time, but they were locked and ready.

"Forget whatever happened. Let's just go back inside," I said. I wanted to reach out and grab his hand, but I knew better. I'd been there—just as locked and ready, waiting for the right moment to fire off. "We came all this way to win, right?"

Deuce's chest rose and fell a few times.

"Ready?" I asked.

Deuce didn't answer at first; then he nodded.

"Let's get to the boards," I said.

We started back toward the center.

I couldn't believe that had worked. I matched my pace to Deuce's, and we walked inside the doors of the convention center together.

CHAPTER FORTY

"Can y'all cut out the drama and get in here?" Twyla was standing right inside the main doors to the convention center. Her voice was on a level-nine irritation, but when Deuce didn't throw back a smart answer, she looked at me with a question mark in her eyes.

"The drama is done." I gave her a little nod. "Let's get to it."

Deuce still didn't answer, but he straightened out his name tag and walked back into the tournament room.

Junior, Mr. Dennis, and Twyla's mom were waiting at the back of the room, looking over the schedule. Everybody seemed calm. Maybe Twyla was the only one besides me who'd noticed the argument between Junior and Deuce. Or maybe everyone else was used to Deuce blowing up.

"All right, young people," Mr. Dennis said, waving

us over. Then he read from a paper. "After they go over the rules, Lawrence, you'll be at table number three; your opponent is David James. Deuce, you'll be at table number eighteen against Harrison Taylor. Twyla, you're at table number twenty-three against Greyson Stills."

"Take a deep breath, say a prayer, and kick some butt," Junior said. He flashed me his gold tooth and then looked at Deuce, who had turned his back completely to Junior and put some space between himself and the rest of us.

I was relieved when a man in a chessboard-patterned suit jacket walked to the front of the room. He welcomed everyone to the tournament and went over the same rules Mr. Dennis had already told us. I took Junior's advice and breathed as deep as I could. Like if I could have dug a six-foot hole and gotten air from it, I would have.

Players, parents, and coaches listened and nodded. Some took notes; some looked around the room, probably trying to scope out the competition.

My head was starting to clear when I heard a voice beside me say, "Watch where you're stepping." It was Deuce talking to some curly-haired white boy who looked like he'd just bumped into Deuce on purpose.

"What you gonna do?" the boy said with more attitude than he looked like he'd have.

"What you say?" Deuce asked, matching the boy's energy.

Don't answer. Don't answer, I wanted to say. No one else acted like they could hear what was going on—hopefully this kid would keep it moving.

"You heard me." This kid had attitude. Was he serious? Right now was not the time to try Deuce. Not that any time was the right time to try Deuce, but right now was *really* not the time.

"Hey, it's nothing." I moved over to stand in between Deuce and Curly Head. I had no problem being the pawn trying to protect Curly from Deuce.

"Nah, he got something to say, he can say it," Deuce said. He stepped closer to me, which was also closer to Curly.

"All you're gonna do is scream at me like you did to that guy earlier." Curly gave a little laugh.

That was it. Deuce flew by me and pushed Curly. Not a regular push—a push strong enough to put Curly on his butt.

A blur of people crowded around Curly. Another blur of people grabbed Deuce.

Oh no, oh no, oh no. Not now.

In less than two seconds, I was yanked out of the way and knocked to the floor.

I couldn't get into trouble right now. Not with Ma and Granny trusting me to come all the way to

Charlotte without them. This was *not* part of the story I was going to tell.

The blur turned into a swarm of raised voices.

I heard Deuce saying, "He started it—he bumped into *me*," while he was being taken out of the tournament room and into the hallway. I was scrambling to my feet when Curly's name tag landed by my hand: HARRISON TAYLOR.

The kid going up against Deuce in the first round.

CHAPTER FORTY-ONE

Disqualified.

Kicked out.

Deuce had lost the game before it even started.

After he'd flattened Curly, he was taken to a time-out room until security could find who was responsible for him. Thankfully, I got to my feet and made it to the time-out room before Junior or Mr. Dennis did.

Security stood guard at the door while Deuce and I waited in silence for the punishment. After our whole team was in the room together, the head chess guy came in and dismissed Deuce from the tournament without any questions about who'd even started it. But I'd seen Curly smirk after he bumped into Deuce the first time.

Deuce and Junior were escorted out of the convention center by security.

It wasn't fair at all—Harrison had wanted this to happen. It felt like that pattern of wrong Ma said Pop was caught in. Chess was important to Deuce; he wouldn't mess up his first tournament for just nothing. Sometimes, even when you're trying to do the right thing, something bad comes your way. And why didn't Deuce get to have *his* story be true? Why was he automatically wrong and Harrison automatically right?

Then Chessboard Jacket turned to me and Twyla and gave us a wide-eyed warning about how we'd be next if we couldn't "follow the rules and handle yourselves accordingly." I had to look real hard to make sure this guy hadn't morphed into Mr. Spacey.

"You can address me, not them," Mr. Dennis said, moving to fill the space between him and us.

"These two can play if they can control themselves," Spacey Jr. said. Then he stomped back into the tournament room.

It was like my last fight at Andrew Jackson was replaying itself, but with no punches by me.

"Put your game faces on," Mr. Dennis said, looking into my eyes and then into Twyla's. "We will not let them see us fold."

CHAPTER FORTY-TWO

The first round of matches was about to start when we got back to the tournament room. I paused at the door before going inside. My stomach churned. We—me and my stomach—had to get it together; it was time to compete.

Table number three was where I had to go. I zeroed in on the table signs . . . great, number three was on the other side of the room. I'd have to snake through a sea of judgy faces to get there. My feet sank into the floor.

Twyla walked up behind me and hummed a familiar rhythm into my ear. Pop's music. I felt my stomach soften a little.

Pop had shown up right on time.

"Let's do this for Deuce," I said to Twyla.

With her head high, she swayed to her table, cool as ever.

David, my opponent, gave me the meanest up-down he could when I got to the table. I didn't care. This wasn't about David or Curly or whoever else came at us. In that moment, I was the smooth lyrics over a funky beat. This was about me, not anyone else, and I felt that freedom Pop talked about. Freedom from everyone staring and thinking all the wrong things about me, freedom to make my own music, and freedom to tell my own story however I wanted to tell it.

"I thought you got kicked out," David said when I sat down across from him. His nasty look was all I needed to see.

I was about to let this kid know there was more to me—the real me—than he thought.

I kept my eyes locked on the board and got ready to battle—not with my fists or my words this time, but with my mind instead. *Chess is a game for thinkers, and I am a thinker.*

David clicked the start button.

It was on.

The rhythm of the game was fast. David was no-where as good as he thought he was. His first move was predictable. So was his second. I countered the third, too.

I was controlling the beat now.

David was getting flustered, moving without thinking. Then he whispered, "I can't let *you* beat me."

Never talk during a match.

He was about to get cooked.

Forty-three moves in, David finally heard my voice for the first time: "Checkmate."

CHAPTER FORTY-THREE

I did it! Playing in the rec was one thing, but playing against this kid who thought he was better than
me was a whole other thing. I felt ten feet tall on my
way back to the spot where Mr. Dennis and Twyla's
mom were waiting—twenty feet tall! I'd won my first
game—in a real tournament, in Charlotte.

I felt like I could lift the entire roof off the building.

"Great match," Mr. Dennis said.

I couldn't wait to tell Ma and Nik. I couldn't wait
to tell Granny, either.

Twyla won her first round too. I could tell by the
way she walked toward us. The Carver Rec kids hadn't
come to play around.

• • •

My electric buzz was back. I was ready for my next match with someone named Charity Rankins.

Twyla was going up against Curly—surprise, he hadn't gotten kicked out like Deuce. Curly had no idea what he'd gotten himself into, playing against Twyla. I knew she'd take him down, for Deuce.

This next level of competition was legit. Charity was good, really good. I held my own, but then she hit me with something that looked like a checkmate trick from Twyla's book. I knew I was gone after that.

Charity was actually nice, though, and whispered, "Good game," after "checkmate."

Even though I'd lost, it felt pretty awesome to have her compliment my game.

Twyla had apparently beaten Curly like it was nothing, because she was already back waiting with Mr. Dennis and her mom when I joined them.

"This next game will be stiff," Mr. Dennis told Twyla. "Remember to think about your opponent's next possible moves before you make your play."

There were fewer players now. The one-and-out games meant only the best were left.

Twyla was quiet and focused as she walked toward table thirteen.

My electric buzz had turned into nervous ants.

I wondered what Deuce was doing. Junior was probably lecturing him about losing his temper and getting disqualified. I wished I could've stopped Deuce from making that last move.

I couldn't see around the room good enough to peep how Twyla was doing. But when she walked back over to us after just twenty-five minutes, I knew it wasn't a win.

"It's all good," she said. "He had some tricks I've never seen before." She was just as cool as she always was. "I took some mental notes. I'll be ready next year."

And I believed her. I'd be ready too.

Mr. Dennis smiled and led us into a group hug. "We showed up, competed, and gave our best," he said. "I'm proud of both of you."

CHAPTER FORTY-FOUR

The drive back to Larenville was a quiet one. Not a cool quiet. Not even a hot, sticky quiet like I'd grown to like in Old Blue. It was a heavy, thick quiet.

The adults weren't talking. Twyla slept while Deuce pretended to sleep and I stared out the window. And even though I'd won a game in my first real tournament and part of me still felt taller than any building in Larenville, I was worried about my friend.

Those two opposite feelings pulled at me the whole ride. A weird tug-of-war. I was happy about my and Twyla's wins, but was playing it down for Deuce. Deep inside, I'd wanted us all to celebrate together.

We made it back to the rec center and went our separate ways.

Mr. Dennis and I drove to Polk Lane. He walked

me up to the front door to greet Granny. Nik and Ma were home too. "Hey, Tracey," he said to Ma, and then to Granny, "You'd have been proud of him, Mae."

• • •

"I won a match at my first tournament!" I said to Nik, Ma, and Granny.

"Lawrence won! I knew you'd win! I knew it!" Nik cheered.

I told Nik, Ma, and Granny what Charlotte was like. I went heavy on the burgers, milkshakes, fried pickles, and fancy hotel, and light on Deuce getting kicked out of the tournament.

I didn't have to play down my happy with them.

When it was time for dinner, Granny called me into the kitchen to help. Before I even got to the door, I saw it.

A new table!

Big enough to fit four chairs—perfect for me, Nik, Ma, and Granny.

"You like it?" Nik came into the kitchen.

Like it? I loved it. "It's just right," I said.

"It'll fit Ivy and Iris, too, if we all squeeze in," Nik said.

They could definitely fit, and I wouldn't even mind breaking up their food fights if I had to.

"We have something for you." Ma handed me an envelope.

"Something else?" I asked. The table was enough.

"Go ahead and open it," Granny said.

Nik couldn't hold her grin inside. And then I couldn't either.

```
Lawrence McDonald has been accepted to the
Booker T. Washington Center for Excellence
in Education for the upcoming school term.
```

For real? Me? "How?" I asked.

"I thought a new environment would be nice," Ma said. "And with all the good you've been doing here lately . . ." She paused.

Then Granny said, "You've really turned things around."

I really had.

I'd made it through a lot. Pop leaving. Moving three times. Being expelled. Pop gone. Ma hardly being around. But I'd had some good come my way too. Actually, I'd *made* some good things come my way. Mr. Dennis had given me a job at the rec. I had more friends than I'd ever imagined I'd have here. Chess had gotten me to stop and think about my next move before doing something silly. And even though Twyla wasn't into the whole boyfriend-girlfriend thing, she was still my friend (at least I hoped so), and now I'd have a new start at Booker T.

I was looking forward to getting back to the rec. I had some things I needed to say to Twyla and Deuce.

CHAPTER FORTY-FIVE

The chess room at the rec was empty on Monday. All the kids were playing a too-big game of dodgeball. It was normally tournament day, but with the big tournament done, I had a feeling the chessboards would be put away for a while.

I asked Twyla to meet me in the empty room. This time I'd be honest—not that I hadn't been honest before, but I'd use my own words, with no gassing from Deuce.

She strolled into the room with a book tucked under her arm.

"Hey, Lawrence," she said with an extra dose of cool.

Her chill vibe versus my sweaty palms made me nervous, but I needed to get this out.

"I'm sorry, Twyla," I started. "I did want to be your boyfriend, or I *thought* I did. Really, I just like you a lot and I wanted to show you that." My throat was a little lumpy, but my words were coming out just fine this time. "Being your friend is all I need," I continued. I wished I had known that sooner. "If you still want to be my friend?"

I hoped she'd say yes this time.

"Of course I want to be your friend," she said. A smile slid across her lips. "We're good." She walked over to give me a side hug—then she punched my arm and said, "Give that to Deuce when you see him."

Her touch sent a small wave through me; she could punch me all she wanted. I didn't think Deuce would get off so easy.

He and I needed to talk.

• • •

Deuce didn't show his face at the rec until Wednesday.

He crept into the chess room, trying to hide out. Whatever was eating away at him had swallowed him whole. I didn't blame him for wanting to be by himself, but I needed to know what was going on.

"What happened?" I asked after we were both in the room alone.

He knew right away what I was talking about. "I don't know," he said. "I just blanked."

"That boy was trying to get you off your game, and

you fell for it." I thought back to what Twyla had said to me after my fight with Deuce when I first got to the rec. "He wasn't worth it."

"My head was all messed up after talking to my mom . . . and I just flipped," Deuce said. "She's staying at a home for people just getting out of prison, and she wants to talk all the time now."

"You don't want to talk to her?" I asked. I'd have given anything to talk to Pop.

"It's not that. . . . It's that she's acting like everything's normal. It's not. And I'm tired of acting like it is. Things aren't the same. I'm not the same."

"I get it." And I did. I remembered how much I had wanted to be a normal family. I'd already figured out normal wasn't real. Still, that didn't stop anyone from wanting it. "Maybe you can tell her what you just told me. She's been gone and you've changed. So there's more to you than she might remember. I'm sure she can understand that."

There was definitely more to me than people saw. I'd figured that out too. I was more than the kid who moved around a lot. I was more than the troublemaker who got into fights. I was more than my pop being gone. I didn't want to be trapped in that history.

"I have something to give you," I said to Deuce. "This is from Twyla." My punch was light enough to make him laugh.

"I messed up, huh?" Deuce asked. I could tell he was really asking that question to himself. "That kid got in my head."

"Don't worry about him. Twyla handled it."

Deuce laughed. "I'll make it up to y'all . . . and to me. I'm better than that. What's that thing Mr. D is always saying about thinking about your next move?" He paused a moment. "Yeah, next time I'll be at my best."

And then I saw him. Not like he hadn't been there the whole time, but for the first time, I saw Deuce without all the hardened skin.

I cranked up my iPod, handed Deuce an earbud, and let Pop's music take us on a trip—in a Cadillac on Vogues, arms leaning out the window, heads bopping with the beat. We were us, Deuce and Lawrence, the coolest dudes in Larenville.

I'd go home later, eat salmon patties and rice just like every other Wednesday, watch *Jeopardy!* with Granny and Nik, and tell them all about my day. I'd fall asleep in Ma's bed with Pop's music in my ears.

Once upon a time, there was a boy called Midnight who was as dark as the night sky, and even though I was still writing my story, I knew for sure it would be mine to tell.

AUTHOR'S NOTE

Thank you for reading *Not an Easy Win*! I'm thrilled to share this story with you.

While this is a work of fiction and there are many parts of this book that bring me joy and laughter, there are components that remind me of some difficult things in my own childhood.

At times, I lived in a multigenerational home, just like my main character, Lawrence. I also grew up with a parent who was absent and often incarcerated. Getting to know Lawrence brought back moments of embarrassment and shame from my own early life. As a young person, I couldn't quite articulate what was happening, and I never felt comfortable discussing my feelings. In part, I wrote this story for young readers who feel invisible or who are holding on to things that bring them shame, because that was me, too.

I wanted to give you, dear reader, an up-close view

of some of the challenges Lawrence deals with and how those challenges affect how he feels about himself and how the outside world views and treats him. I also wanted you to see Lawrence win—at chess, at finding a caring circle of friends and family, and at understanding how to tell his own story.

If you are experiencing some of the same challenges Lawrence does in this book, I'd like to offer you encouragement and give you permission to be the author of *your* own story. You can be more than who society expects you to be.

I see you and believe in you.

With love,
Chrystal

ACKNOWLEDGMENTS

The sophomore book struggle is real, y'all, and during a pandemic no less. I learned a lot about myself as a writer and as a person during the creation of this book—I am better because of it.

My sincerest thanks to some very special people:

My lovely agent, Elizabeth Bewley, who always has my back and is a seamless combination of encouraging and realistic. We are perfectly matched.

My brilliant editor, Shana Corey, who is a champion for my work and always pushes me to greater heights. Thank you for believing in my vision for this world and these characters and for helping me transfer those details from my mind to the page all while keeping their heart.

I'm grateful to the whole team at Random House Children's Books: Tia Resham Cheema, Polo Orozco, Kathleen Dunn, Noreen Heritz, Dominique Cimina,

Alison Kolani, Barbara Bakowski, Karen Sherman, Janet Foley, Erica Stone, Emily DuVal, John Adamo, Kelly McGauley, and Michelle Nagler. The School and Library team: Adrienne Waintraub, Kristin Schulz, Natalie Capogrossi, and Shaughnessy Miller—thanks for being amazing and so supportive.

A big, big thank-you to Katrina Damkoehler for designing the cover and Xia Gordon for the absolutely stunning cover art.

Many thanks to Chess NYC for your expertise; any errors are mine and mine alone. Special thanks to Jasmine W. for your sensitivity notes.

To my friends and critique partners: Maria Frazer, Dorothy Price, Ife Nellons, Leigh Anne Carter, and Becky Shillington, your support is more than I could have ever asked for. Thank you for checking in again and again. Every call, email, and text message meant more than you know.

Chad Lucas, you are the only person I trusted with the earliest version of this book—thank you for your honesty and reassurance.

A huge thank-you to the21ders! We are family forever.

To every teacher, librarian, blogger, reviewer, bookseller, and reader who has ever supported me and my work—thank you!

To my mother and my sister, who listen to all my

random rambles about the publishing world, thank you for continuing to believe in me.

My first and most special inspiration is my son, Ezra, for whom I continue to write.

Lastly, my deepest gratitude to my husband, Jeremy, for your endless encouragement, support, and cultural expertise (ha!) and for being the best hype man.

ALSO BY CHRYSTAL D. GILES

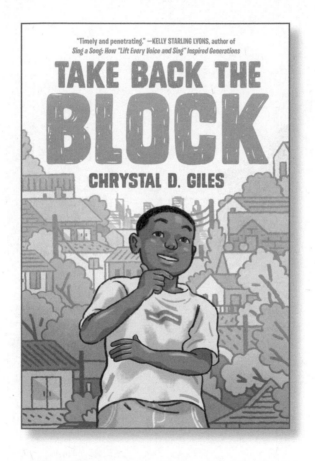

"Timely and penetrating." —KELLY STARLING LYONS, author of
Sing a Song: How "Lift Every Voice and Sing" Inspired Generations

TAKE BACK THE
BLOCK

CHRYSTAL D. GILES

SOME THINGS ARE WORTH FIGHTING FOR!

ABOUT THE AUTHOR

Chrystal D. Giles is a champion for diversity and representation in children's literature and made her debut with *Take Back the Block,* which received multiple starred reviews and was an NPR Books We Love selection. Chrystal lives outside Charlotte, North Carolina, with her husband and son and is currently working on her next middle-grade novel.

chrystaldgiles.com

 @creativelychrys

@chrystaldgiles